AGAINST THE CLOCK

Samantha Baca

Dark Shadows Series

Five Steps Ahead
Ten Seconds Too Late
Against The Clock

Content Warning:
This book contains language and storylines that may be bothersome for some readers and is intended for a mature audience. Violence and sexual scenes may be shown in detail as well. The reader is encouraged to reach out to the author directly (authorsamanthabaca@gmail.com) if they would like to further discuss the content warning(s) for this book.

Please note the following items that come up briefly in the book:

Violence
Child loss (mentioned briefly)
Child Abuse (mentioned briefly)
Sexual Assault (mentioned vaguely, not in detail)
Child Trafficking

Contents

One: Quinn...1
Two: Roman - 14 Days Ago.....................................3
Three: Quinn - 14 Days Ago.................................13
Four: Roman - 13 Days Ago.................................17
Five: Quinn - 11 Days Ago...................................25
Six: Roman - 11 Days Ago....................................29
Seven: Quinn - 10 Days Ago................................37
Eight: Roman - 10 Days Ago................................43
Nine: Quinn - 9 Days Ago....................................49
Ten: Roman - 9 Days Ago.....................................55
Eleven: Quinn - 9 Days Ago.................................61
Twelve: Roman - 9 Days Ago................................67
Thirteen: Quinn - 8 Days Ago..............................73
Fourteen: Roman - 8 Days Ago............................77
Fifteen: Roman - 7 Days Ago................................85
Sixteen: Quinn - 7 Days Ago................................89
Seventeen: Roman - 7 Days Ago..........................95
Eighteen: Quinn - 6 Days Ago............................101
Nineteen: Roman - 6 Days Ago..........................105
Twenty: Quinn - 6 Days Ago...............................109
Twenty One: Roman - 5 Days Ago......................115
Twenty Two: Quinn - 5 Days Ago.......................119
Twenty Three: Roman - 5 Days Ago....................123
Twenty Four: Quinn - 4 Days Ago......................127
Twenty Five: Roman - 4 Days Ago......................133
Twenty Six: Quinn - 3 Days Ago.........................139
Twenty Seven: Quinn - 3 Days Ago.....................149
Twenty Eight: Roman - 3 Days Ago.....................151

Contents

Twenty Nine: Quinn - 2 Days Ago....................153
Thirty: Roman - 1 Day Ago....................161
Thirty One: Quinn - 1 Day Ago....................165
Thirty Two: Roman - 1 Day Ago....................169
Thirty Three: Quinn - 11 Hours Ago....................173
Thirty Four: Roman - 2 Hours Ago....................179
Thirty Five: Quinn....................183
Thirty Six: Roman....................185
Thirty Seven: Rosie....................187
Thirty Eight: Quinn....................191
Thirty Nine: Roman....................195
Forty: Quinn....................199
Forty One: Roman 203
Forty Two: Rosie....................209
Forty Three: Quinn....................213
Forty Four: Roman....................219
Forty Five: Rosie....................223
Forty Six: Roman....................227
Forty Seven: Quinn....................231
Forty Eight: Roman....................241
Forty Nine: Quinn....................245
Fifty: Roman....................249
Epilogue: Quinn - 4 Weeks Later....................253
Other Books by Samantha 259
Acknowledgments....................263
About the Author....................265

<u>One</u>

Quinn

The front door swung open, the rain spraying in from the wind that whipped past. I turned my head, knowing that Roman was back from messing with the generator but felt my body stiffen when I saw five figures dressed in all black, wearing ski masks, rush through the door.

I jumped off the couch, startling Rosie as I tried to shield her with my body. I reached behind for my gun, panic crushing over me when I remembered it wasn't there. It was unlike me not to have it on my body, but I had been distracted after I got out of the shower right before Roman went outside to prepare for the storm that was already upon us.

"NO!!" I shouted, shoving against the bodies as they charged us. I felt strong arms grab me and fling me to the side as Rosie screamed from the couch. I got up and swung at the masked figure in front of me, watching as their head shot to the side from the impact of my punch, but it wasn't enough. Someone held me by the waist, ensuring that I couldn't get to Rosie.

Panic flooded through me as I tried to get free. It was useless, and I knew it. We were outnumbered and I was unarmed—biggest fucking mistake of my life.

I could hear Rosie scream and turned my head toward the sound right as someone picked her up and tossed her over their shoulder. A black pillowcase was shoved over her head as they rushed out the door. I continued to fight against the strong arms holding me in place, desperate to get to my daughter. My pulse raced and my breathing was erratic as adrenaline pumped through me.

I tried to turn to see where they had gone, the front door still wide open. There was a black van parked right outside, and I immediately recognized it. Seconds later, the back door was slammed shut before it sped off, the sound of gravel crunching beneath it.

I tossed my head back, feeling the sharp pain as I made contact with a head, eliciting a loud growl from the recipient. It wasn't enough to knock him out, but it did piss him off to where he tightened his grip around my throat, making it harder to breathe. I brought my hands up and tried to pry his hands away, desperate for air.

Roman will be back any second. He'll come save me. He'll take me to get Rosie back. Then we'll kick ass and take out everyone who's ever tried to hurt my daughter. She's only five years old...

But before Roman could get there, a hand reached up and covered my mouth with a towel. Everything turned black, and the voices around me faded.

Two

Roman

14 Days Ago

I tilted my head back and felt the cold chill as the beer slid down my throat. It was hot and muggy, making the buttoned-down white shirt stick to my body. The music played loudly throughout the backyard as lights lit up the dance floor where a handful of women in super short dresses were dancing.

I didn't have to look at them to know that they were watching me. Each time the song changed, they would glance at me over their shoulder as they rubbed their hands up and down their body and thrust their hips along to the beat. There was so much effort put into each move, and I couldn't find the energy to try to engage any of them.

There was only one woman who had caught my attention tonight, and it fucking sucked because there was no way that I could talk to her. It wasn't like I was shy or didn't know *how* to talk to women. It was because she was my best friend's little sister, and I knew that he would kill me if he knew the thoughts going through my head every time I looked at her.

Quinn wasn't anything like the other women around us. Her raven black hair was pulled into a loose ponytail, high up on her head, and she looked comfortable in a pair of jeans and a t-shirt. She didn't wear the club outfits, or the heavy makeup that Mike's cousins were wearing—who I was informed *weren't* off-limits when I tried to get out of having a drink with one of them. She also looked more relaxed than the handful of FBI agents that lined the wall with their water bottles clutched to their chest, leaving wet marks on the silk dress shirts they probably wore every day, even outside of work.

I knew I shouldn't be so judgmental about the people Mike worked with, but it had kept me entertained for the past hour as I studied everyone at his birthday party and decided who was family, who was a coworker, and who was the unfortunate soul lucky to be considered a friend—me.

Mike didn't want a big party for his birthday, but his baby sister, Sonia, decided they needed to have one. His mom gave in, and they put together a big bash in her backyard and told him he had to invite a few friends. Sonia had handled the rest of the guest list—which explained why half of their cousins and other distant relatives were there.

"Why don't you come dance with me, Papi?" one of his cousins—I had no fucking clue what her name was—asked me, breaking me out of my trance as I stared at Quinn while she spoke to her daughter, Rosie.

"Na, I don't dance," I lied, leaning back to avoid being too close to her.

"It's okay, I can teach you," she purred, reaching for me with the longest red nails I had ever seen.

"He doesn't need dance lessons," Mike cut in, stepping around her to take the seat next to me. He handed me a beer and rested his ankle on his knee. "He's the best dancer here."

This made her eyes light up as my eyes narrowed in his direction.

"Go on, *Papi*," he taunted, nodding toward the dance floor. "Show her what you're working with."

I was about to open my mouth to object when I spotted Quinn being led to the dance floor by Rosie.

"Fine," I muttered, setting my beer bottle down on the table between us. I got up and took her devil claw as she shimmied her hips toward the dance floor.

Once we were on the wooden deck with everyone else, I tried to force a smile as she looked at me over her shoulder while grinding her ass against my groin. Quinn turned in time to see it, her cheeks splitting while she tried to contain her laughter. She pulled her lips together in a thin line and held her hand in the air as she twirled Rosie a few times.

It only took half a turn before she spotted me and released her mom's hand to rush over to me.

"Dance with me?" she asked, putting her hands together in front of her as she begged. I smiled down sweetly at my favorite "niece," thankful that she had just saved the day.

"Sorry, I can't say no," I said to the devil woman and turned to Rosie before she could object. I caught a brief glance of her flicking her long, dark red hair over her shoulder before stomping off in her stripper heels.

"You saved me, kiddo," I said to Rosie as I held her hands and danced with her.

"Yeah, you looked super scared," she giggled. "Mommy says we should always help people when they need it."

"Your mommy is right," I agreed, looking up at Quinn as she watched us.

I spun Rosie around, noticing how much she looked like Quinn with her dark hair and brilliant blue eyes. Quinn's eyes were a light shade of blue that sometimes turned gray, like Mike's, but Rosie had more of her dad's sapphire blue eyes that made them absolutely mesmerizing. I dreaded the day when she was old enough to date, knowing that Mike would have his hands full as an overprotective uncle.

We danced for a few more minutes until the song ended,

and Rosie declared that she needed a drink of water. Quinn was about to go with her when her mom held up a hand and waited for Rosie to join her before leading her into the kitchen.

"Do you want to dance?" I asked, holding my hand out and hoping she would take it.

"Sure," she smiled, letting me pull her into me as we moved our hips to the salsa music.

People who *really* knew me knew that I loved to dance. When we were younger, I was always known as the life of the party because I couldn't sit still. It didn't matter what kind of music it was—I was moving.

Tonight was different, though. Maybe it was the gentle breeze that brushed past us and caressed our hot skin, or maybe it was how Quinn's petite body fit perfectly against mine. Either way, I didn't want to stop or let go. The song changed, and I looked up in time to find Sonia watching us with a mischievous grin as a slow, sexy song started playing.

I felt Quinn's body tense slightly with the way I held her and thought about pulling away some so I didn't make her uncomfortable.

"I can't remember the last time I danced like this," she said nervously, tucking a stray strand of hair behind her ear.

"Me neither," I agreed. But it wasn't because I didn't dance much these days; it was because I had never danced with someone who made me feel what I was feeling while holding Quinn.

"I don't think Justin and I even danced like this at our wedding," she laughed, then looked away. I knew that it was still hard for her to talk about him after he died tragically on the job. Justin was also in the FBI—witness protection, just like Mike, though they rarely worked together.

I didn't know what to say, so I stayed quiet and gently rubbed my thumb soothingly over her back.

Her mom came out of the kitchen a few minutes later without Rosie. I noticed her at the same time that Quinn did. Suddenly, she pulled away from me, her hands still gripping my biceps as her eyes rapidly scanned the backyard.

"Where is Rosie?" she asked, panic heavy in her voice.

She spun around, standing on her tiptoes, trying to get a better view.

"Let's go ask your mom," I offered, gently leading her that way with my hand on her lower back.

The party was still going with people packed into the small backyard. We wedged our way through until we reached Sandra.

"Mom, where's Rosie?" Quinn asked, grabbing her arm to spin her away from the older man she was talking to.

"She's inside using the restroom," her mom answered, her brow furrowed in response to Quinn's tone.

"By herself?" Quinn muttered angrily before rushing inside.

I followed behind her, ready to help with whatever was upsetting her.

She rushed through the kitchen, bumping shoulders with a few people before she started pounding on the bathroom door.

"Rosie! Open the door," she yelled.

A few minutes passed before she pounded again.

"Rosie—" she started but was cut off when Rosie came out of a bedroom with a man behind her.

"I'm right here, Mom," she said.

Quinn's eyes widened as she looked between the two of them.

"What were you doing?" Quinn asked, reaching for her daughter and pulling her out of the man's grip as he rested his hand on her shoulder. She squatted in front of her and held her hands.

"I needed the bathroom, but someone was in it. So then I went to Grandma's, but I couldn't figure out how to get the door to close because it was stuck. Uncle Saul heard me and came to help me."

Quinn stood up and tucked Rosie into her side, facing me instead of the man she was calling Uncle Saul.

"You only have one uncle, Rosie, and that's Uncle Mike. We don't go anywhere with someone we don't know, understand?"

"Yes, ma'am," Rosie replied quietly, tucking her chin.

"It wasn't a big deal," *Uncle Saul* said. "I didn't want her wandering around by herself, so I popped in to check on her."

"Thank you," Quinn said through clenched teeth. "In the future, she needs to come find me instead."

"Hey, no harm, no foul," he laughed and held his hands up while Quinn shot daggers through her eyes. He walked by and patted Rosie's head before getting lost in the crowd.

"Mom, can I go outside again?" Rosie asked, tugging on her arm. "Uncle Mike is right there."

Quinn turned her head and nodded as Mike gave her a quizzical look. He reached his hand out and waited until Rosie took it before leading her outside.

I stood by Quinn and noticed how her fingers trembled

while she closed her eyes and let out the shaky breath she had been holding.

"What's going on, Quinn?" I asked, gently touching her arm.

She crossed her arms tightly over her chest and avoided looking at me.

"Nothing," she lied.

"Bullshit," I hissed out quietly to avoid drawing attention to us.

Her brow raised.

I folded my arms over my chest, matching her, aside from my chest being much broader and more muscular than her feminine one that I was trying hard not to stare at.

"It's my job to read people, and I can tell that you're lying."

When she continued to refuse to answer me, I let out a heavy sigh and tilted my head to look at her.

"Just tell me what's going on, Quinn."

"I can't."

"Why not?"

"Because I can't."

I paused for a moment, trying to figure out the best way to approach this. I knew Quinn well enough to know that once she shuts down on something, there's no coming back from it. Something was going on, and I was determined to find out what it was.

"If the US Government thinks that I'm trustworthy, surely you can too," I offered with the smile that usually got me whatever I wanted.

For a split second, she looked like she was considering telling me before she snapped her jaw shut and pulled her shoulders back.

"It's getting late. I need to get Rosie home."

She didn't look back as she stormed out and found her still with Mike, dancing happily in the grass. I followed after her but kept my distance, watching as they made their way to his mom to say goodbye. She frowned and looked disappointed but could tell by Quinn's face that it wasn't the time to press her to stay.

They slipped out quietly, with Quinn keeping a hand on Rosie's shoulder the entire time, almost like she was afraid to let her out of her sight. I walked over and sat down next to Mike in the same seats we were sitting in earlier. I scanned the crowd noticing it had started to thin out some.

I looked down at my watch. It was barely after ten, but apparently, people our age didn't party as hard as we did twenty-some years ago. I spotted the guy who had been with Rosie in her grandma's bedroom and was about to ask about him when I heard Mike mutter, "who the fuck invited her?" before slouching down in his chair and pulling his Yankees ballcap lower over his face.

"Nice to see you too," the woman said with fake enthusiasm, hitting the side of his arm with her tiny purse. I knew it had an official name, but I could care less what it was.

"To what do I owe this pleasure?" Mike asked, looking her up and down before getting bored and looking away.

Whoever she was, was dressed nicely in a black dress wrapped tightly around her body, showing off some major curves. Her black heels gave her an extra four inches, making her look even taller than she already was.

"I'm here to meet someone," she replied. She looked around as Mike stood up, then seemed to notice me. Not wanting to be rude, I joined them and extended my hand to hers when she said, "I'm Anastasia."

"Roman," I said, biting the inside of my cheek when I

realized exactly who she was. "It's so nice of you to join us for Mike's big birthday bash." I clapped my hand on his shoulder and felt him elbow me in the ribs.

"Well, given that I know how much he would enjoy that, I'm not here for it." She laughed lightly and looked around. "I'm supposed to meet someone here, but I don't see them."

"Meet someone?" Mike asked, head tilted to the side. "Like as a *date*?"

I watched the blush creep up her neck.

"If you must know, yes, like a date."

"Dressed like that?"

"What's wrong with how I'm dressed?" She planted a hand firmly on her hip.

"Nothing, it's just a little…" Mike threw his hands in the air when he couldn't think of the words he wanted to use.

"Sexy?" she offered with a smug smile.

"There you are," a man interrupted, bumping my shoulder as he squeezed his way between Mike and me to hug her. "Are you ready to go?"

"I sure am," she replied sweetly, almost flinching when he slid his arm around her waist.

"Cool," he said heavily, the smell of beer heavy on his breath. "Happy birthday, man. See you on Monday."

As they left, I felt my stomach knot tighter when I watched *Uncle Saul* walk out with Mike's archnemesis from work.

"Who is that guy?" I asked, nodding to them as they left.

"Saul, he works with me. So does Satan's mistress."

"I've heard a lot about Anastasia," I laughed. "But you

never mentioned that she's fucking hot."

"She's not hot," he scoffed and furrowed his brow. "She's an annoying pain in the ass who gets in my way instead of helping."

"Sounds like you like her," I teased. "Maybe you should ask her out?"

"Over your dead body," he grunted.

"Isn't it supposed to be over your own dead body?" I asked.

"Not with her. She's like a fucking cat, and there's no escaping once she digs her claws in. I'd have to use your dead body as a barrier first."

Three

Quinn

14 Days Ago

I sat on the bed, gently rubbing Rosie's head even though she had already fallen asleep. Tonight had been unnerving—to say the least—but then I had to deal with her massive meltdown on the way home from my brother's birthday party because she wasn't ready to leave.

I was used to always being the bad guy; it came with the territory of being a single mother. But it was hard, and some days it wore on me more than others. Today was one of those days.

My head laid against the pillow I had tucked behind me an hour ago when we first came in here, and I got her settled in for the night. She had stopped crying and didn't bother to tell me what a terrible parent she thought I was for making her leave tonight. She didn't have to, I could see it in the sadness in her eyes long after the tears dried.

Mike had texted me shortly after we left to make sure we were okay, and I wondered if Roman had said something to him. They were best friends, so I never knew where I stood in the equation. While Mike was my older brother and would do anything to protect me, Roman was also like a brother to me, and I trusted that he wouldn't say anything to him if he didn't know what was going on. He never struck me as the kind of person to gossip or discuss something he didn't have all of the facts about. It was probably from his time in the Marines, but Roman was one of those people who sat silently until they decided it was time to take action.

I had replayed the night over and over in my head the entire train ride home, and long after Rosie fell asleep. I knew that it would be hard to see some of Mike's coworkers at the party tonight. I hadn't seen most of them since Justin's funeral four years ago. Even though I worked for the FBI, we never crossed paths, and I loved to believe that fate played an important role in that. That maybe after everything life had given me over the years, I was finally going to be one of those people that nice things happened to.

I picked up my phone and found another text message from Mike and one from my mom. Neither of them seemed as worried as Roman, so I felt comfortable knowing that he hadn't said anything to them.

I replied quickly, pretended that I was tired, and lied that I was calling it a night soon. Instead, I kissed Rosie's head and quietly crawled out of her bed, making sure the nightlight was on.

I crept down the hallway, praying that the squeaky floorboards wouldn't wake her up. I ventured into the kitchen and poured myself a glass of wine, stopping halfway when I remembered that I could no longer afford the luxury of being buzzed. I needed to be alert and aware at all times from now on.

With my small glass of wine, I headed into the living room and sat down, tucking my feet beneath me. I grabbed my laptop and got settled in, not sure what I was even looking for.

When I woke up this morning, I expected it to be like any other day—eat a quick breakfast, get Rosie ready for school, spill coffee on myself at least once before I got into the office, and then listen to my boss complain all day about how incompetent women were since I was the only female in our department.

The day had gone almost as expected until I picked Rosie up from school. People were usually scattered in the pickup line on Friday, so I had parked on the street and gone in to get her. While I was waiting for her to finish talking with her friend, one of the teachers approached me and asked if she could speak privately with me.

I had expected to hear something about how Rosie had exceeded their expectations on a project or had gone out of her way to help another student. That was just the wonderful type of girl that she was. Instead, she pulled me into a classroom and exchanged nervous glances with another teacher, who confirmed she would watch Rosie for me.

Once we were by ourselves, she pulled her cell phone out of her pocket and handed it to me. There was a video on the screen, and my stomach sank when she pressed play. I was nervous and anxious to see what it was since she wasn't acting excited or happy about it. At first, it showed kids playing on the playground, then it zoomed in to focus on the man standing across the street, leaning against a black van with dark windows.

He was of average height and build, wearing a baseball cap that hid his face and dark sunglasses covering his eyes. Everything about him looked casual, from the way he crossed his ankle over the other to how he tapped his cigarette against the side of the van and let the ashes fall. But I knew better.

I swallowed hard before I handed her phone back to her, unable to get any words out.

Someone had been there, casing the playground. A pervert was lurking in the shadows, watching the innocent children as they ran around and played without a care in the world. MY child had been there, unaware of the danger not even fifty feet away from where she was playing.

When I finally found my voice, I asked why they didn't call the cops when they saw the man watching the kids. Her face fell with her shoulders, and she watched the video again.

"At first, we thought that he knew Rosie because she was the

only one that he was watching. But when she looked in his direction a few times and didn't seem to recognize him, we knew that wasn't the case. We called the police, but we're still waiting for them to send someone out...."

Her words had gone in one ear and out the other at that point. I was beyond furious, but I couldn't figure out which part had me fuming the most. The fact that someone had been there watching my daughter or the fact that I wasn't there to do anything about it. I had to trust that she was safe at school, and suddenly, it didn't feel like she was safe at all.

Four

Roman

13 Days Ago

"How was Mike's party?" Trevor asked as I pressed the phone against my ear.

"Fun, uneventful," I shrugged even though he couldn't see me. "I just got to his mom's house to help take the tables and chairs back that his sister rented."

"So basically, you ended the night early and were in bed before midnight?" he teased.

"Hey, I'm almost forty. I can't handle the long nights of drinking and partying anymore. I'm not young like you."

Trevor laughed, and we both knew that it was a stretch to say he was still young, given that he was usually in bed before me most nights, and he was barely thirty.

"Did you at least meet any nice girls?" he prodded.

"Now you sound like my mother."

"Well, she has a point. You're not getting any younger. Soon that mythological super sperm you claim to have will be all dried up, and you won't be able to give her any grandbabies."

"You're just as ridiculous as she is," I laughed. "Now, is there a reason for your call, or did you just want to ruin my Saturday?"

"I was calling to let you know that I won't be in on Monday. Max needs to pick up some stuff for the wedding, but the only store that has it is in New Jersey, so I'm going to go with him to help."

"Not a problem. I'll get one of the new guys to cover the front desk and have Jackson run the floor while I take care of the admin stuff."

"Thanks, brother. I appreciate it."

"Hey, that's what a *partner* does," I laughed, then hung up and tucked my phone into my pocket.

It was barely eleven in the morning, but the day was already scorching hot. Instead of my usual button-down shirt and jeans, I opted for a t-shirt and shorts this morning, knowing that I would just get sweaty with moving stuff.

I hadn't seen Mike yet, so I headed for the house, assuming he was already there and probably convincing his mom to make biscuits and gravy for him. He was a total mama's boy, and she was a sucker for her only son—a win/win for them most days.

I knocked on the security door before hearing someone yell to come in. I went inside and wiped my shoes on the welcome mat before heading in the direction of the savory sausage I smelled coming from the kitchen.

"Aren't you going to lock the door?"

I whipped around to see Quinn standing behind me. Her brows were pulled together, her hair knotted in a messy bun on top of her head. Without makeup, I could see the faint dark circles under her eyes and wondered if she had had a rough night last night.

"Sorry," I muttered, turning to lock the door. When I looked back at her, her brows were raised while she waited for me to slide the deadbolt in place.

My fingers moved slowly as her eyes followed every movement until the door was securely locked.

"Better?" I asked.

"Thank you." She nodded and tucked her head.

"No problem."

I followed her into the kitchen, smiling when I saw that I was right about Mike conning his mom into cooking for him. She was standing at the stove with a pink paisley apron tied around her waist while she turned sausage in the skillet.

"Good morning, Mama Sanchez," I said as I gave her a quick hug from behind and kissed the top of her head.

"You know you can call me Sandra," she laughed, shaking her head. "Twenty-some years later, and you're still so formal. Even my own kids aren't that formal unless they want—"

She turned around and pointed her spatula at me.

"What do you want?" She narrowed her eyes playfully, trying not to smile as I held an empty plate out to her.

Her resolve finally crumbled when she took the plate and laughed, loading it with a generous serving of scrambled eggs, hash browns, sausage, and gravy from the different pans scattered on the stove. I thanked her before eagerly taking it and finding a place at the table. I hadn't bothered to say hi to anyone before I reached in and grabbed a few biscuits from the pan in the center of the table.

"Good morning to you too," Mike said around a bite of food.

"It's a great morning," I teased, lifting my fork in salute to his mom. "Thank you again, I'm very spoiled this morning."

"Thank *you* for coming to help clean up from the party and take all of those tables and chairs back," Sandra said with a sigh. "Sonia has good intentions but lacks in the follow-up part of most things."

"Be sure to chew your bites so you don't choke," Quinn whispered to Rosie before pulling her hair behind her back so it was out of her precious little face.

"I will, Mom," Rosie replied before popping a sausage link in her mouth and chewing it.

Quinn sat down next to her and picked up her coffee, bringing the mug to her lips but not bothering to take a drink. I could tell that she was distracted by something, but I didn't want to ask in front of everyone.

Suddenly her eyes lifted to mine, and she slightly flinched when she found me studying her. She took a drink of coffee and then pulled her phone out of her pocket. With her head down, I couldn't see her face anymore, so I went back to eating my breakfast.

Once we were done, we helped clean up while Sandra sat down with Rosie and ate her breakfast. I washed the dishes while Quinn dried them, not bothering to look at me. Everything about her felt oddly robotic this morning, and I couldn't shake the feeling that something was wrong.

"What do you have going on today?" Mike asked as he put the leftovers in the fridge.

I looked over my shoulder and found him watching Quinn. Her shoulders stiffened before she turned slightly to answer him.

"I have a couple of errands that I need to run."

"Like what?" he pressed.

"Personal stuff."

"Momma is going shopping for new clothes for me," Rosie volunteered, smiling as she took a bite and chewed.

"New clothes? For what?" Sandra asked, joining the conversation.

"School," Quinn said sharply, gripping the plate in her hand so tightly that I worried she might break it.

"I thought she had enough school clothes? Besides, school will be out in a few weeks."

"She just needs new clothes, that's all."

"Did they implement a new dress code?" Sandra wondered aloud. "You would think that they would wait until the new school year starts before they do that. I mean, you can't be expected to buy a new wardrobe for her when she'll be out on summer break soon anyway. Who knows if she'll even fit in the same clothes when she goes back."

I could feel the tension radiating off of Quinn as she dropped the plate and didn't bother to try to catch it.

"Enough!" she yelled, her fists clenched by her side. "*I'm* buying her new clothes because *I* don't want her wearing skirts and dresses to school anymore. It's my choice. My decision. I'm 38 years old; I don't need anyone bossing me around or trying to tell me what to do."

She turned around and met Rosie's eyes that were welling up with tears.

"I can't wear my pretty dresses anymore?" Rosie cried. "Do I have to dress like a boy now?"

"No, sweetie," Sandra said, pulling her against her chest. "We all just need to calm down for a moment and figure things out. Why don't you go clean up and get that syrup off of your face before Charity gets here?"

"Okay, Grandma."

Rosie padded down the hall to the bathroom while the kitchen filled with silence.

"What in the world is going on, Quinn Marie?" Sandra asked, standing up with her hands on her hips.

"It's nothing, Mama," Quinn sighed, leaning against the sink.

"Then why are you not letting her wear dresses and skirts anymore?"

She took a deep breath and ran her hands down her face before answering.

"Her teacher showed me a video yesterday when I went to pick her up. It was of the kids playing during recess, but when she zoomed in, there was a man across the street watching them. He was leaning against a black van with dark windows."

"Oh, for heaven's sake," Sandra whispered and covered her mouth.

"That's not the worst part," Quinn said quietly, looking down the hall to see if Rosie was heading back. "The teacher said that the only kid he was watching was Rosie."

I felt the air rush out of me. Mike was sitting at the table with his jaw clenched and fists tight. I knew the feeling—I wanted to find whoever this bastard was and smash his face as bad as he did.

"I know that this is your job, honey," Sandra said softly, "but making her wear pants isn't going to stop whoever this is from looking at her."

"I know," she whispered. "I feel helpless right now. I don't know what to do or how to protect her, which is really fucking frustrating given that I do this for a fucking living. I work for the FBI in the child exploitation task force—I literally see this stuff every day, yet I don't know what to do."

"It's always different once it hits close to home," I assured her, though I had no idea. I had been a sniper in the Marines, so nothing ever hit too close to home for me.

"We'll figure this out and find a way to protect her," Mike said, pushing away from the table and standing up. "For now, I'm going to go outside and pack up the tables and chairs while I work off some of this newly found anger."

I gave Quinn one last look before going outside to help Mike. Even though Quinn wasn't a child anymore, that didn't stop me from wanting to protect her the same way I had growing up. She was only a few years younger than me, and I knew she could handle herself. She had been proving that ever since her husband died four years ago. So why did I suddenly have such strong feelings to help her with this?

Five

Quinn

11 Days Ago

The morning had started rougher than I would have liked for a Monday. Rosie had thrown a fit when I presented her with a stack of pants in different prints and shirts that would match them instead of the skirts and dresses that she loved to wear. It was a battle that lasted long enough for her to rush through breakfast and caused us to be late getting her to school.

We hurried through the empty hallways as I swung open the door to her classroom, looking frazzled and out of sorts as her teacher came over to check on us. Rosie rolled her eyes before flinging off her backpack and taking her seat at her desk. The students looked over their shoulders and whispered before the other teacher got their attention and refocused them on whatever they had been working on before we got there.

"I'm so sorry she's late," I said, blowing a strand of hair out of my face. "We had a rough morning. I'll stop by the front desk before I head out."

"It's alright," Miss Gentry said, holding her hands up. "We'll get Rosie caught up, she didn't miss much."

I blew out a heavy breath and looked around at the class of innocent children who were smiling and laughing at something one of the kids had said.

"We'll keep her safe," she promised, pulling my attention back to her.

"If anything happens, or if you see anyone who looks suspicious, please call me on my cell. I can get back here quickly."

I opened my purse and fished a business card out of my wallet. She took it and smiled, tucking it safely into her back pocket. I turned and slipped out the door, taking one last look at Rosie before it shut behind me.

The front office was polite and made a note of why Rosie was late. I made sure they had my cell phone number, as well as my mom's, just in case they needed to reach me. I thought about giving them Mike and Sonia's numbers, but they already looked annoyed that I was spending so much time obsessing over every little detail in her file that I thought better of it and left.

As I walked out, I scanned the streets around the school, focusing on where the van had been parked in the video. I studied everything around me—trees that would provide a hiding spot in the thickness of their branches, buildings with narrow alleys small enough for someone to stay in the shadows and not be seen, and businesses with storefront windows that created the perfect opportunity to watch the school without being noticed.

I felt uneasy as I made my way to work, wondering how many other dangers were constantly lurking around her school. It was hard enough being a parent and worrying about your children in an ordinary world, but I found that it was even harder when you worked in a field that consistently showed you how cruel the world is and how ready monsters are to take your children from you.

By noon I had checked my phone at least a hundred times, looking for any missed calls or text messages from Rosie's teachers. Her class would be getting out soon, and my mom had confirmed that she would be there to pick her up. Typically I would be the only one to drop her off and pick her up, but my boss had called a mandatory last-minute meeting that just happened to be at the same time that I needed to leave to get Rosie.

I wanted to Facetime my mom and watch to make sure they got home okay, but I couldn't. Not only would that piss my boss off during his meeting, but it would also make my mom even more worried about me and my newest obsession with keeping Rosie safe.

It wasn't just the video that had gotten under my skin—it was this feeling deep inside of my gut that told me something was wrong. I had learned to trust my instincts a long time ago, and they weren't just hinting that something might be wrong—they were *screaming* that something was very wrong.

I hadn't been able to shake the feeling, which had led to sleepless nights and dark circles under my eyes that didn't hide well even with the heavier makeup I had worn this morning. The meeting was supposed to start in fifteen minutes, so I shoved the rest of my protein bar into my mouth and grabbed a notepad and pen from my desk.

The conference room was already half full, so I took a seat toward the back and pulled my phone out to find a text message from my mom.

The corners of my lips turned up into a smile as I looked at the picture of Rosie and my mom at her house, sitting on the couch in front of the window. The blinds were open, allowing the sunlight to flow in.

"Good afternoon," my boss said as he entered the room and took his place at the head of the table. I was about to put my phone away so I could concentrate, but suddenly I saw something in the picture that sent a chill through my body.

My fingers trembled as they pinched then zoomed in on the photo. Across the street was a black van with dark windows and a person sitting in the driver's seat.

<u>Six</u>

Roman

11 Days Ago

I was thankful that it was slow at work because with Trevor being out of the office and Jackson calling in sick, it left me running around trying to be in multiple places at once. The gym wasn't usually busy on Mondays, which allowed me to work on some of the admin stuff from the front desk. I had a few clients on the schedule, but I had been working with them for so long that they didn't really need a personal trainer anymore. I knew that they would get started with what we had been working on and wait for me to come guide them through the rest.

By the end of the day, I was wiped and ready to crash out. I stopped by the market store on the corner, grabbed a few things for dinner, and headed home. It was just me, and even though I liked to eat healthy, it didn't mean that I was great at keeping groceries in the house. I made note to do some shopping this weekend and stock up so I didn't have to see the barely legal teenage girl in the lowcut shirt and googly eyes that always seemed to be working when I went to the market.

I climbed the three flights of stairs instead of taking the elevator and walked down the hallway to my apartment before stopping short. Standing outside my door were Quinn and Rosie, huddled together as if she was trying to shield her from something. Panic started to rise as I quickened my pace. Something had to be wrong for Quinn to just show up at my apartment.

"Quinn?" I asked stupidly, but I still couldn't believe she was there.

She spun around and looked at me, a protective hand reaching behind her to keep Rosie in place.

"What's going on? Is everything okay?"

"Do you think we could go inside and talk?" she asked nervously.

I nodded and unlocked the door, holding it open for them to enter before I pushed it closed and slid the locks into place. I set the paper bag down on the kitchen counter and put my hands on my hips, unsure of what to do.

"Is it okay if I turn the TV on for her?"

Rosie stood in front of Quinn with Quinn's hands wrapped protectively over her shoulders. Her brows were raised while she waited for me to answer her question.

"Of course." I shook my head to clear some of the fog while I turned on the TV and flipped through the channels until I found something that seemed appropriate for Rosie to watch.

Once she was settled on the couch, I went back to the kitchen to talk to Quinn. It was an open layout, with the kitchen and living room blending into one large room, which allowed us to keep an eye on Rosie.

"Is everything okay?" I asked, arms folded across my chest and my voice barely above a whisper.

"I don't know," she admitted and let out a shaky breath. "I keep trying to tell myself that all of this is in my head and that I'm freaking out for no reason."

"But?"

"But I don't think that it's nothing. I think someone is actively watching Rosie, and I'm afraid that they're going to take her."

She swallowed the last few words as silence fell between us. I looked over my shoulder at the little girl sitting on my couch with hair as dark as her momma's and a smile that could light up the dimmest room.

"You have to trust your gut," I agreed. "What happened?"

"My mom had to pick her up today because my boss called a mandatory meeting last minute, and I couldn't go get her. I think that my mom knew how stressed out I've been since her teacher showed me that video on Friday, so she sent me a picture of them sitting together on her couch once they got home."

She stopped talking and looked past me to Rosie. Her eyes filled with tears that she tried to blink away before they fell.

"When I zoomed in on the photo, I saw the same black van from Friday parked across the street."

"Fuck," I exhaled and ran a hand over my face. "Have you told anyone about this?"

She shook her head.

"I don't want them to think I'm crazy if I'm wrong about this."

"And what if you're right?"

"That's what I fear the most. I can't be with her 24/7, and if someone is watching her, they will know my schedule and when I'm not around. They'll know exactly when to take her."

She chewed her bottom lip, popping it free when she caught me watching.

"So, what's the plan?" I asked, desperate for a distraction from her mouth. "How can I help?"

"I really hate to ask," she hesitated. "But do you think we can stay here tonight while I try to figure out what to do? I haven't slept since I found out on Friday, and I don't think

I'll get any sleep tonight knowing that they followed her to my mom's house."

I wanted to say *absolutely, you can take my bed, and I'll sleep on the couch*—but I knew I couldn't. It wasn't that I didn't want to help Quinn—I would give my life to protect her and Rosie. Hell, I would give a vital organ or two to protect Mike, but this was different. I needed to know that he would be okay with me helping and letting them stay with me because if he found out on his own, it wouldn't go over well.

"You know that I don't mind helping you, Quinn, but why not go to Mike?"

She sighed and let her shoulders fall.

"I knew you would ask that," she laughed.

"He's my best friend," I replied lightly. "I can't imagine that I would be so easygoing if he went behind my back to help my sister and niece if they were in trouble and he didn't tell me."

"That's not fair; you don't even have siblings."

"True," I said, raising a brow. "But *if* I did, I would want to know what was going on."

We stood there silently for a few minutes while Rosie laughed at something on TV.

"It's not that I don't trust my brother to protect us, but I feel like I need space to think about things. I know that once he really knows what's going on, he'll be obsessive and trying to take over to where I can't think straight. You guys are two totally different people. Yes, he's strong and had training, but not the same as you had in the marines. You both have a different skill set, and if someone's coming for my daughter, I know that you can put a bullet between their eyes before they even see you."

"I'm not a sniper anymore," I countered, feeling my shoulders tighten.

"It's not something that you lose. You and I both know that. I've seen you play darts with Mike, and you don't miss a single one."

I rolled my neck, trying to alleviate some of the tension.

"It's just one night, Roman." She held her hands in front of her. "Please."

Rosie's innocent laughter floated through the air, and I knew what I had to do.

"Fuck," I muttered on a breath, closing my eyes.

"I promise we won't be in the way. You won't even notice us."

I bit the inside of my cheek at the thought of being in the same apartment as Quinn and *not* noticing her. That was like watching a giant meteor come crashing toward Earth and not understanding how you got knocked out when it hit you.

"Fine," I said sternly. "But I have some conditions that I will not budge on."

"Okay, whatever you want."

Don't fucking go there.

"First—I'm going to order pizza, and you guys are going to eat. Second—you two will sleep in my bed, and I'll take the couch. Third—I will go with you to drop her off at school in the morning." I paused before adding, "and no matter what, you will tell me if anything happens that I need to know about. If you see something, hear something, smell something— anything that feels off—I need to know about it right away. Deal?" I held out my hand and waited for her to take it.

She started chewing her lip again, not bothering to shake my hand.

"Can we compromise on the bed part of it?"

"No."

"Roman," she sighed. "I do not want to put you out and make you sleep on the couch. We'll be fine sleeping in the living room."

"First of all, you're not putting me out. I'm offering it. Second, you're not both going to fit on the couch, and there's no way in hell that I'm letting you sleep on the floor."

"But—"

"No, Quinn. Those are the conditions. Either take them or leave them. If not, I'll call your brother and tell him what's going on."

She narrowed her eyes at me and folded her arms across her chest.

"You wouldn't."

"Try me."

I took a step toward her, encroaching on her space enough to feel the heat radiating off her body. I wanted to reach out and touch her, caress the soft skin on her face and assure her that everything would be okay.

She shook her head and let her arms fall.

"Fine, you've given me no choice. I accept the conditions and thank you again for letting us stay here."

"You're welcome," I replied, ignoring the tingles that rushed through me at the thought of having Quinn stay the night with me.

It took Rosie telling Quinn that she was hungry before we snapped out of the trance that we had fallen into and stepped away from each other.

"How does pizza sound?" I called over to Rosie, taking a breath of Quinn-free air as I tossed the stuff from the paper bag into the fridge. Even if a five-year-old was on board with sushi, I didn't have enough for everyone and still lacked the groceries I would need to make something edible for dinner.

"Can we get extra pepperoni?" she squealed excitedly.

"Is there any other kind of pizza?" I joked, pulling my phone out of my pocket to call in the order.

Seven

Quinn

10 Days Ago

I woke up around three o'clock this morning, unsure of where I was and why the pillow smelled so delicious, like a combination of cedarwood and vanilla. Once I remembered that I was sleeping next to Rosie in Roman's bed, everything from the day before came flooding back to me.

I inched down the hall to use the restroom, hoping not to wake him up, when I found him sitting on the couch with his laptop. He looked like he had tried to go to bed at some point since he was wearing a t-shirt and athletic shorts. I started to worry that maybe we had kept him up or that he couldn't sleep because the couch was too uncomfortable when he turned around and caught me watching him from the hallway.

I tugged at the flimsy shirt that barely covered the length of the booty shorts that I liked to sleep in. I had packed a quick bag of overnight clothes for Rosie and me before we came over and new outfits for the morning, but it was hard to find the right combination of comfortable and appropriate. It was early June and already getting hot and uncomfortable, so I liked to sleep in as thin of layers as possible.

"Everything okay?" he asked, turning his body to take me in. His voice was gravely, like he had been sleeping.

"Just got up to use the bathroom."

I walked into the living room so he didn't have to strain to see me.

"Sleepless night or uncomfortable couch?" I asked, praying that I wasn't inconveniencing him and causing him not to get sleep tonight. I felt bad enough for coming here, to begin with, but I didn't know what else to do.

"I slept for a few hours and then got up for a drink of water. Something kept bothering me about the picture you sent me, so I got my laptop out to do some research."

That immediately piqued my interest, and I found myself sliding down onto the couch beside him. I tried to make sure I kept my distance so I didn't make him uncomfortable, but it was hard not to touch him since he was sitting in the middle of the couch instead of on one of the ends.

"What did you find?"

"In the picture, the person in the driver's seat of the van is wearing a baseball cap," he said, grabbing his phone and zooming in on the picture. "I knew that I recognized the logo but couldn't figure out why. I searched for the image, and it comes up as the logo for a little league baseball team."

He turned the computer toward me, and I immediately recognized it.

"That's for the Astros. It's the little league team that Rosie played for last year. Mike coached it until she decided to quit."

"It could be a borrowed hat, but I think it's worth looking into to see if it gives us a lead into who's been watching her. Especially if it's the same team she used to play on."

I nodded my head, completely speechless.

"It's going to be okay," he assured me, gently squeezing my hand.

I flinched momentarily at the contact but not because I didn't want him to touch me. Instead, I felt myself leaning in toward him, desperate for more. There was something about the way that my body felt like it was on fire where his fingers touched me that had me longing to feel him elsewhere.

As if reading my mind, he slowly pulled his hand away and closed his laptop.

"I should get back to bed before Rosie wakes up and freaks out that I'm not there," I stuttered, standing up and almost tripping on the rug.

"Okay," he said before I rushed out of the room and to the bathroom. I peed quickly and then climbed back into the bed, thankful that Rosie had stayed asleep.

I rolled onto my side and watched her for a while, memorizing every little detail on her face the same way I had when she was born and again when Justin died. I hadn't realized just how much I had taken for granted being able to look at him when I wanted to or feeling the comfort of his embrace when I needed it. I promised myself that I would never allow that to happen again and that I would try to soak up every single moment, regardless of how little it seemed at the time.

A few hours later, I woke up to the sunlight filtering in through the curtains and rolled over to check the clock on the nightstand beside me. It was just after six, and I needed to get up and shower before I woke Rosie up.

Slowly I rolled out of bed and grabbed the duffle bag from the floor before tiptoeing down to the bathroom. I didn't bother going to the living room to see if Roman was up yet before I opened the bathroom door and went inside. I quietly shut it behind me, not noticing that the light was already on before I turned around and found Roman wearing nothing but a towel wrapped around his waist.

His brown hair was still wet from the shower, and his tanned, muscular body glistened beneath the water beads.

"Oh my God!" I whispered loudly, my heart nearly jumping out of my chest. I covered my eyes with my hand, dropping the duffle bag to the floor. "I'm so sorry! I should have knocked first!"

"It's fine, Quinn," he chuckled. "You can open your eyes. I'm not naked."

"It's okay," I laughed nervously. "I can just go so you can finish up."

I turned to open the door, not bothering to uncover my eyes, and hit my arm on the knob.

"Son of a bitch!" I tried not to yell, so I didn't wake Rosie, hoping that the sound of me whacking the door hadn't already stirred her.

There was shuffling behind me, and then I felt his hand on my shoulder as he pulled my hand from my eyes.

"It's safe," he teased.

I opened my eyes and found him wearing a fitted t-shirt and joggers, which looked ridiculously good on him.

"Is that what you wear to train people?" I blurted out as my eyes traveled over his body again.

"Um, yeah?"

He pulled his lower lip between his teeth, watching me as he waited for my eyes to finally land on his.

"Sorry," I muttered. "I didn't mean to stare."

"Are you sure about that?"

Was I? Because I was pretty sure that had he not busted me checking him out, I would probably be fantasizing about him teaching me how to do some sort of sexy pull-up at the gym.

I lowered my head and looked away as I felt the heat creep up my neck and spread across my chest.

"The shower is all yours," he said, extending his arm in that direction. "There are towels under the sink. Be careful with the water—it gets hot pretty quickly."

He smirked and walked out, closing the door behind him. I couldn't be sure, but I was pretty positive there was some sort of sexual innuendo laced in his comment.

Eight

Roman

10 Days Ago

The morning started differently than I had anticipated. First off, I woke up with a stiff neck from sleeping on the couch. Second, I was overly exhausted from the lack of sleep because my mind was going a mile a minute. And third, I couldn't shake the excitement that I felt when Quinn walked in on me in the bathroom.

Thankfully, I had already showered and was covered when she burst in, but that didn't stop my dick from stirring at the sight of her skin blushing as she tried to look away. Had Rosie not been there, I probably would have entertained dirtier thoughts than I already had.

While Quinn showered and got ready, I started a pot of coffee and searched through my cabinets to find something suitable to make for them for breakfast. I couldn't imagine that many five-year-olds began their day with protein shakes, and I definitely didn't have any sugary cereal or Pop Tarts lying around.

Rosie woke up right before Quinn came out and stumbled into the living room, rubbing her eyes as she tried to wake up.

"What time is it?" she asked sleepily.

"Just after six-thirty," I answered and poured myself a cup of coffee.

"Do I have to go to school today?"

"I can't imagine why you wouldn't."

"I don't want to." She sat down on the barstool beneath the counter and pouted.

"Why not?"

"It's boring, and we don't do anything fun. I would rather stay here with you."

"Well, I don't get to stay home today. I have to go to work."

Speaking of which, I still needed to text Trevor and let him know that I would be late this morning. I hadn't talked to Quinn about it yet, but I was also planning to escort her to work after we dropped Rosie off at school. I knew that Quinn wasn't worried about herself right now because Rosie felt like the only threat, but I wasn't willing to take any chances.

"Will I have to work when I'm an adult?" Rosie asked as I finished my text message and pressed send.

I set my phone down on the counter and smiled as Quinn walked into the room.

"We all have to work," Quinn answered, sliding past me to snatch the other cup of coffee from the counter. "And you need to go brush your teeth so we can get going. I'll grab you breakfast on the way."

"But Mom," she whined.

"But nothing." Quinn brought the mug to her lips, the steam billowing over the top. Her eyes narrowed as her brows raised. Rosie plopped off the barstool with a loud sigh and shuffled down the hall to the bathroom.

"They say it's supposed to get easier the older they get," Quinn sighed before taking a sip. "I find that hard to believe."

"I can imagine," I laughed. "She's a great kid, just a whole lot of her mama's sass in that little, tiny body."

"Hey," Quinn protested with a chuckle. "That's not all me. Justin contributed some too."

"Yeah, the good stuff. Like doing well in school and listening to anyone but her mom. It reminds me of someone I knew who was an unruly and rebellious teenager."

She groaned and closed her eyes, holding the cup between both hands.

"Oh, God. It's only going to get worse, isn't it?"

We both knew that she was joking, but the realness of her words was enough to shut both of us up.

"Sorry, I was going to make breakfast, but I didn't think she would be on board with a protein shake."

"She probably would have been all for it. I, on the other hand..."

"I can treat this morning," I offered with a smile. "I know this great bakery that's on the way to her school. We should have plenty of time to stop if we get going soon."

"*We?*"

"We talked about this when you agreed to the conditions, Quinn. I'm not budging."

"Sorry," she sighed with resignation. "I guess it couldn't hurt to have more eyes on her and the school."

"Exactly why I came up with the idea, to begin with," I winked.

I turned to put my empty cup in the sink at the same time she turned to walk into the living room.

"Sorry," she said as our chests collided, the hot liquid in her cup almost sloshing over.

My hand darted out to grab the cup before it could spill and burn her, but her grip only got tighter and left me holding her hand. Our bodies were touching, the heat between them almost electrifying.

"You okay?" I asked gruffly.

"Mmmhmm," she mumbled, refusing to look up at me but also refusing to pull her hand away.

We stood there for a few seconds, waiting for the other to make the next move when Rosie suddenly returned.

"What are you guys doing?" she asked, pulling her backpack on over the clean t-shirt she had changed into.

"Nothing," Quinn answered, her voice a higher pitch and shakier than normal. She set her cup down on the counter and wiped her hands on her dress slacks. "Let's finish getting ready so we can go."

They went back to the bedroom to gather their stuff while I tried to focus on what I needed before we left. My mind had never been as scattered as when Quinn was around.

The drop-off at school was uneventful, which we had assumed it would be. Quinn fought me on making sure she got to work safely but finally gave in and let me. By the time I got to work, Trevor was studying me like I was some sort of alien, given how late I had gotten there.

"Sorry, I'll make up the hours," I said as I slid into my chair and sat down to get started.

"Don't worry about it. I was late this morning too."

"Everything okay?"

I turned on my computer and waited for it to start so I could check my schedule for the day. Typically I would know my schedule for the entire week, but today, I barely knew my name.

"Yeah, Elena wasn't feeling well."

"Again?" I raised a brow.

"I think she has what Hannah had."

I scrunched my face, remembering how sick he had mentioned she had been.

"I hope she feels better soon," I offered, while also praying that he didn't catch it and bring it to the office with him. The last thing that I wanted or needed right now was to get sick.

I checked my phone a few times, relieved when there weren't any calls or texts that Rosie was in danger, and then got to work. Maybe today could be a productive day after all.

Nine

Quinn

9 Days Ago

"Let's go!" I yelled over my shoulder. It was hump day, and there was nothing that I wanted more than to be humped. Okay—maybe that was a bit dramatic, but I imagined it would put me in a better mood than I had been in.

Yesterday had gone by like any other day after we left Roman's house in the morning—aside from him going with us to drop Rosie off at school and then insisting that he escort me to work. We checked in with each other a few times throughout the day, but there was nothing to report because everything felt back to normal again.

This morning I woke up with a borderline migraine, likely caused by the lack of sleep that I had gotten last night. I hated that the only good sleep I had recently was when I slept in Roman's bed and pretended that it was his body that I was cuddled against instead of the pillow that smelled like his body wash. Not that I had lathered myself up with it in the shower the morning I got ready there.

When there was nothing to report after Rosie got home from school and no vans were seen hiding in the shadows, I told myself that everything was fine and there wasn't a reason for us to stay with Roman again. Sure I had felt safer being there with him, but that didn't mean I needed to inconvenience him more than I already had.

"I can't find my shoe," Rosie called from her bedroom.

"Can you just put on another pair?" I yelled back, feeling bad for losing my patience. I didn't feel like fighting with her this morning, especially over a pair of shoes.

"These are the only ones that don't make my feet look weird in these pants," she whined, coming into my bedroom holding one shoe in her hand.

"Fine," I sighed, getting up from the bed and smoothing down my skirt. I glanced in the mirror to make sure that I had managed to put on matching heels before I followed her into her room to look for the lost shoe.

We got to school thirty minutes late, and this time, the front office wasn't as friendly and welcoming as it had been on Monday.

"I'm so sorry—it won't keep happening. I promise."

The older woman with a pencil sticking out of her bun gave me the stink eye before writing on a piece of paper and sliding it to the side.

"Tardiness has never been a problem for Rosie before," she said with way too much judgment in her voice. "If this continues—"

"It won't," I interrupted, holding my hands up.

I didn't bother sticking around to exchange pleasantries with any of the other office staff, given they all seemed just as grumpy and in need of a mid-week hump day.

By the time I got to work, my boss had given me the same disapproving look before I slipped past his office and hid in mine. I hadn't had time to eat and didn't bother to grab anything on the way since I was already late. It felt like life was more stressful this week, and I hated the feeling of things being out of control.

I grabbed my blue light glasses from my drawer and slipped them on, ready to start the day.

Just then, my phone vibrated with a text message. I let out a heavy sigh as if this was the break I needed from a long, stressful day that hadn't started yet.

Roman: How are things this morning?

Me: Fine. Chaotic. The usual?

I found myself chewing the inside of my lip, unsure of what to say. The last thing I needed was for Roman to worry that I wasn't okay. *But was I really okay?*

Roman: Do you need anything?

Me: That's a loaded question.

Roman: Anything that your brother wouldn't kill me over?

I brought my fingers to my lips and tried to hide my laugh. Was he flirting with me? Deep down, I really hoped that he was.

Me: I wouldn't worry about Mike. He's just always angry because he should be hooking up with his partner instead of constantly fighting with her.

Roman: Anastasia?

Me: I think so?

Roman: The woman from the party that left with the creep from the bathroom?

I frowned and tried to think of who he was talking about.

Me: Creep from the bathroom?

Roman: Uncle Saul.

Me: Oh, that guy.

God, I hated that guy. I had never felt comfortable around

him from the moment I met him. Justin didn't care for him much either, but they worked together, and right before Justin died, they had been assigned to each other as partners.

Me: She left with him?

Roman: Said she had a date. Mike seemed pretty pissed about it.

Me: Because he secretly wants to bang her.

Roman: I don't think I want to hear about your brother banging anyone.

Me: Yeah, I don't think I want to talk about it either.

Roman: How was Rosie this morning? Did she get her donut for getting an A on her spelling test yesterday?

I lowered the phone to my desk and held my head in my hands. Damn it! I knew I had forgotten something this morning. That also explained her sudden hostility toward me on our way to school.

Me: No, there was a shoe incident, and we were late. I totally forgot about it until now.

Roman: I'm sure she'll understand.

Me: Not a chance. Rosie holds grudges more than anyone I know. I worry about her future boyfriends— especially when they cheat on her in her dreams. They're in for a world of hurt.

Roman: Shit.

Me: Right?

Roman: Maybe you can make it up to her and grab them on your way home?

I felt the idea start to blossom inside of me, finally

something good that could turn the day around and get me back on Rosie's good side. Before it could last, I heard the ding on my computer and read the email that had just come in from my boss.

Me: Apparently the universe hates me today. My boss just scheduled another mandatory meeting this afternoon.

Roman: Are you going to be able to make it to pick her up?

Me: No. I'm going to call my mom and see if she can help me again.

Roman: I can pick her up if you want. Just call the school and let them know. I'll be sure to check in at the front desk when I get there.

I felt my heart flutter at the offer. How he even knew the procedures were beyond me, but I didn't have time to stop and question it.

Me: Are you sure? I don't want you to have to miss work.

Roman: I'll just take a late lunch. It's no big deal.

Me: Okay, if you're sure?

Roman: Quinn- stop. I got it.

Me: What about work?

Roman: I can just bring her back here if that's okay? Then I can take her home when you get off.

Me: Okay, but let me know if she starts to be any trouble.

Roman: She's five. How much trouble can she be?

I tipped my head back and laughed.

54

Ten

Roman

9 Days Ago

"Are you sure you don't want anything else?" I asked Rosie as we stood in line with a handful of random snacks. I had no idea what to feed her and didn't want her to go hungry until I dropped her off when Quinn got home from work, so we made a quick stop for reinforcements. Some for her, some for me. I didn't have siblings, so it wasn't like I was used to having kids around me, and to be honest, I was a little nervous being responsible for Rosie for a few hours.

The school didn't give me any problems picking her up, and while I wanted to think that it was because Quinn had already called and informed them, I had a sneaking suspicion that it was because the women in the front office couldn't figure out how to put their tongues back in their mouth long enough to give me any trouble over it. While that was reassuring on some level, it was more irritating given that we were worried someone was watching her, and I hated to think that it would be equally as easy for them to walk in and take her without any questions asked.

"No, thank you." She set her stuff on the counter and smiled at the older woman who started ringing us up.

"Well, aren't you just the prettiest little thing I've seen all day," she cooed, lighting up as she looked from Rosie to me. "You look just like your daddy." She smiled up at me, and I felt my stomach tighten.

"He's not my dad," Rosie replied matter of factly. "My dad died."

"Oh honey, I'm so sorry."

"Can we go now?" Rosie asked, looking up at me with tears in the corner of her eyes.

I nodded and handed the woman my card, not bothering to listen when she gave me the total. I grabbed the bag and led Rosie out, my hand protectively splayed across her back as we headed to the gym.

Trevor had been at lunch when I left to go pick her up but was back in the office when we got back.

"Hello!" she said excitedly as she bounced into the room, shuffling around the back of my desk to climb up into the chair.

"Hi," Trevor replied with a smile that nearly split his cheeks. "How are you, Rosie?"

"You know my name?" She stopped what she was doing as her face dropped in surprise.

"I do," he confirmed. "I also know your uncle Mike, and my buddy Roman was just telling me all kinds of fun stuff about you before he went to pick you up from school."

"Like what?" Her elbows rested on the desk as her head lay in her hands while she waited.

"Hmm, let's see." He tapped his fingers together before widening his eyes and looking from me to her. "He told me that you love superheroes and that Hulk is your favorite."

She gasped before a smile spread tightly across her face. I opened the bag of snacks and spread them out across my desk before grabbing the two protein bars and tossed one to Trevor. He caught it and gave me a nod.

"Hulk is my favorite, but I also love Captain America. He's sooo dreamy," she sighed.

Trevor and I looked at each other and then turned back to her.

She tilted her head back and laughed.

"That's what Grandma Sandra says when we watch the movies. I think boys are gross, but she says that someday when I'm older, I'll change my mind." She opened the small bag of Doritos and fished one out before popping it into her mouth.

I felt a rush of relief wash over me.

"Boys are gross," a voice said from the hallway.

I looked up to find Mike walking into the room, a look of confusion on his face as he looked between the three of us.

"Why is Rosie here with you? Where's Quinn?" he asked, looking around as if I had her hidden under my desk or something.

"She had a last-minute meeting and needed someone to pick up Rosie, so I volunteered."

I kept my answer simple, but I knew he would see right through it.

"Why didn't she ask my mom? Or me?" He furrowed his brow, then narrowed his eyes. "Since when do you and Quinn talk anyway?"

"I…. Ummm…." I looked nervously at Rosie, not wanting to say anything that would frighten her or upset Quinn, given I didn't know how much she wanted Rosie to know right now.

"Hey, Rosie, I need to go check on the guys in the back. Do you want to come with me?" Trevor asked, pushing away from his desk and waiting for her to join him.

I raised a brow at him, silently telling him to keep an eye on her.

"I've got her, don't worry."

Once they left the room, I let out the breath I was holding.

"What the fuck is going on, Roman?"

I could either lie and hope that it didn't ruin our friendship, or I could tell the truth and pray that it didn't ruin the new one I felt was forming between Quinn and me.

"Just spit it out," he said, noticing that I was struggling.

I tilted my head back and looked at the ceiling.

"Fine. Quinn came to stay with me Monday night, and we've been talking since."

There, that wasn't a lie, and it wasn't overindulging in the little details that I wasn't sure if I should be sharing.

"Are you two—" he pinned me with a look that felt a little too murdery for my liking.

"Really? That's what you think she came over for? Rosie was there, for fucks sake, Mike." I shook my head but didn't know if I was more frustrated that he had asked or if I was still feeling overly guilty because I had entertained the thought of doing exactly that several times while she was there.

"So if my niece weren't there, you would have been banging my sister?"

"Is that something you really want to know?"

"Don't fuck with me, Roman," he warned.

"Or what?"

"She's my baby sister, and she's been through enough already."

"And I'm not looking for a random hook-up. You should know me better than that, Mike. Besides—that's not even what it was about. Believe it or not—there are other things to worry about other than whether or not your best friend is doing your sister."

I knew the moment the words left my mouth that I had said too much. His face softened some, but his shoulders seemed to tense beneath the blue dress shirt he was wearing.

"Tell me what's going on."

"You already heard about the incident at school with the van. On Monday, Quinn had another meeting that came up at the same time that she needed to pick Rosie up. Your mom went to get her instead, and she sent Quinn a picture of them sitting together on the couch at her house. Quinn knew that it was your mom's way of putting her at ease to know that Rosie was safe, but when she zoomed in on the picture, the same van was parked outside with someone inside it."

Mike clenched and unclenched his fists a few times while working his jaw. I could tell he was pissed, and I didn't blame him.

"Why didn't she come to me?"

"I asked her the same thing." I sat on the edge of my desk and crossed my ankles.

"And?"

"She was scared, Mike. Really scared. She hadn't slept in a few nights and thought that she would sleep better if they stayed with me because she knew that no one would get into my apartment without me hearing them first."

"I can protect her too," he countered but lacked the conviction in his tone that said he believed it.

"I know. She knows that too. But we all know that my training was different from you guys."

He sighed and plopped down into an empty chair by the window.

"So what's happening now? Why is Rosie really here?"

"It's true that Quinn had a meeting today. She offered to have your mom pick Rosie up, but I volunteered instead. I felt better knowing that I could keep an eye on her if she were here with me."

"Have you seen the van since Monday? Should we be filing reports or something?"

I stood up and walked around my desk to my computer.

"We haven't seen the van since your mom's house. I went with Quinn to take Rosie to school yesterday morning, and everything looked normal. She hadn't noticed anything unusual, and Rosie's teachers are on high alert. They actually had a talk with the kids today about safety and what to do if someone tries to take them. But no, we can't file any reports because it's not illegal to have a van parked outside of a school. We don't have any proof that someone is watching Rosie and nothing to go on. You know better than anyone that all we can do is watch and be alert right now."

"Were you able to identify the driver?" Mike asked, tapping his foot anxiously.

"No, but I was able to zoom in enough to get a logo off of the baseball cap they were wearing. Come check it out."
I stepped back and let him stand in front of me to see the computer. Pulled up was an image of the little league logo.

I handed him my phone, and he played the video a few times, zooming in to see it.

"Unbelievable," he muttered. "That's the logo from Rosie's little league team."

"I know," I sighed. "Quinn told me. We're not sure if it's a parent, a coach, a fan—it could be anyone who happened to find the hat and wear it. Hell—for all we know, it could have been donated, and someone picked it up at a thrift shop. We have no way of knowing where it came from."

Mike handed the phone back to me and shook his head.

"I know exactly where it came from. It's mine."

Eleven

Quinn

9 Days Ago

It felt like it took forever to get to Roman's work, probably because I had this terrible feeling of being away from Rosie all afternoon and not knowing if she was okay. I trusted that Roman would keep her safe, but I also knew he had no idea what to expect from a five-year-old. For all I knew, she had tied him to a chair and painted his nails bubble gum pink while trying to style what little hair he had since it was cut so close to his head.

I shuffled through the door and heard laughter in the back of the gym. I knew the sound of her giggles from a mile away and felt the corners of my lips turning up as I gave the kid at the front desk a quick wave and headed toward it.

"Is that all you got?"

I stopped for a moment before I turned the corner and walked into the room. I knew that voice, but why was he here? Had Roman gotten into so much trouble that he felt he needed to call my brother for backup?

I walked in and stopped in my tracks, holding a hand to my heart.

Rosie was bouncing back and forth in front of a boxing bag, her little hands barely fitting in the gloves that covered them.

"Come on, Rosie, you can do it!"

I looked around, noticing that Roman was standing next to

her, coaching her on where to hit next, while Mike proudly stood on the other side, wearing the biggest grin I had ever seen. There were two other guys in the room, but I didn't recognize them.

She pulled her hand back and then punched with all of her might, her small body looking ridiculously tiny compared to the giant bag.

"That's it, Rosie!" Mike yelled.

I walked over and stood next to Roman, folding my arms over my chest.

He turned his head for a split second, noticing I was there, before turning his attention back to Rosie.

"Okay, how about a break," he said nervously, and I knew he was trying to gauge my reaction.

Rosie spun around, a frown on her face that quickly changed when she saw me.

"Mom!" She ran over and wrapped her arms around me, almost knocking me over. "Did you see me?!"

"I did," I laughed, her excitement enough to make me feel silly.

"He was showing some guy how to hit the bag, and I really wanted to try it. He said no, but then I asked Uncle Mike, and he said yes."

I raised my brows at Mike, who just shrugged.

"Then Trevor jumped in and helped me get the gloves on, and his friend Max came by, and he gave me some pointers too."

"It looks like you're a very lucky little girl who has a whole army of superheroes to protect you," I said quietly, pulling her into me for another hug.

"They talked to us at school today about what to do if

someone tries to take you, but I think that if anyone ever tried to take me, I would just hit them instead."

My heart skipped a beat, and I could feel the heat of everyone's eyes on me.

"Well, let's hope that never happens. Now, go get ready so we can go home and give Roman a break."

"Can we stay the night with him again?" Rosie asked as she pulled her gloves off.

My eyes flew open as I whipped my head around to Mike. There was *no way* that this was going to go over well. I had planned on telling him about it soon; there just hadn't been time.

"Relax, I already know," Mike said, holding his hand up to stop the trainwreck of thoughts pulsing through my head.

"You know?" I looked to Roman, begging for more clarity. Did Mike know about us staying there and nothing else, or did he know about everything else?

"We talked, and there's something that you need to know," Roman said, lowering his voice as he stepped closer. Trevor and Max—I guess were their names—helped Rosie put her gloves away before taking her back to Roman's office to get her backpack.

"What's up?" I asked a little too nervously as I looked between Mike and Roman.

"Remember the hat we saw in the photo from your mom's house?" Roman asked.

"Yeah," I said slowly. I had a bad feeling about whatever they were about to drop on me. "What about it?"

"It's mine," Mike said with a tight smile.

I pulled my head back in confusion.

"It's your hat? You've been stalking Rosie?"

"No," he blew out and rolled his eyes. "But my hat used to be in my office, and I haven't been able to find it for almost a week."

"How do you know it was yours?"

"Because there was a stain on the side from Rosie's peanut butter and jelly sandwich. She was so upset about it and didn't want me to find it, so she got the scissors and tried to cut it off."

"Oh my god," I laughed. "I remember that!"

Roman pulled out his phone and zoomed in on the picture.

"See right there," Mike said as he pointed to it. "That's where it was cut."

I squinted my eyes and held the phone closer. Sure enough, there was the missing chunk. Why hadn't I seen that before?

"So someone stole your hat and is wearing it around town while they watch my daughter?" I asked, flinging my hands in the air. "Why? It doesn't make any sense."

"Someone is targeting her; we know that much for sure," Roman said.

"But Quinn, you're also missing the bigger picture here," Mike added gently. "It's not just *someone*. It's someone who had access to my office and knows a lot about her already."

My blood ran cold as a chill spread throughout me.

"You think it's someone in the FBI?" I whispered.

Mike flinched but didn't say anything.

Suddenly all of the pieces started falling around me. It wasn't just that it was someone in the FBI; it was that it was someone who worked with my brother in the witness protection program—the same department my husband worked in before he was killed on the job.

"What was the last case that Justin was working on before he died?" I asked, forcing my voice to be stronger than I felt.

"Quinn—you know that I can't—"

"Tell. Me."

Mike's shoulders fell, and he looked down at the floor.

"Ariel Wyland. She was a victim of sex trafficking. The only one who went to court and put her captor behind bars."

"Where is she now?" I asked, knowing that he couldn't tell me since she had gone into witness protection shortly after leaving the courtroom.

"The U.S. Marshal's office confirmed they found her body yesterday."

Twelve

Roman

9 Days Ago

"I don't think it's a good idea for you to go home by yourself," I said, gently holding Quinn's arm so she couldn't leave.

"We'll be fine," she insisted, looking around for Rosie's hair tie that she had lost somewhere in my office.

"Don't be so stubborn," Mike cut in, giving her a pointed look. "You know better than anyone what we're dealing with, and now your daughter is the target. Let us protect you."

"So what do you suggest?" she asked, hand planted firmly on her hip.

"You can come stay with me," he offered.

"I don't think that's the best idea," Max said from the other side of the room. He and Trevor had stuck around for a bit after I pulled him to the side to ask him a few questions about what was going on. If Trevor trusted him, my gut told me that I could as well.

"Why not?" Mike responded, turning to look at him.

"Because you're as much of a target as they are. Whoever it is—they're making sure it's obvious that they have a connection to you otherwise, they wouldn't have taken your hat and worn it while sitting outside of your mom's house. That wasn't a slip-up; it was very intentional. Someone is trying to make sure you get a message, and if Quinn and Rosie stay with you, you're putting everyone at risk."

"I agree," I said with a sigh. "It's apparent that this person works with Mike and has access to his office. They probably know where he lives and his routine." I paused and then looked him in the eye. "They'll take advantage of you wanting to protect your family. They want you to be distracted, so you let your guard down. You can't keep them safe and do your job at the same time."

"My job has nothing to do with this," he grunted and ran a hand through his hair in frustration.

"It does," I countered. "You need to be focused at work to figure out who it is. That means you need to be as far away from Quinn and Rosie as possible until we know what is happening. We can't afford to have you distracted and making mistakes."

"I don't make mistakes," he bit out.

"It only takes one, and we can't afford that right now." I rested my hand on his shoulder and squeezed. "I've got them. I promise."

"I'll see if I can get a couple of guys to set up some surveillance," Max offered. "And don't worry—they're good at staying hidden. I'll work out the details with Roman and figure out where we want eyes."

"Not the same guy you had to watch Elena?" Trevor said with a laugh.

"No," Max groaned. "That rookie left and never came back. They're former military, and I trust them with my life."

I nodded and patted Mike before going over to my desk to grab my stuff.

"If you need to take a few days off," Trevor offered as he grabbed his things as well.

"Thanks, but I'm good. I think it's best if we keep

everything as normal as possible. We don't want to do anything to spook them before we figure out who it is."

"That still doesn't solve the problem of Quinn going home by herself," Mike said. "I don't like her being there alone with Rosie, knowing that someone is watching them."

"They can stay with me tonight," I replied, noticing the faint blush that crept up the side of Quinn's neck.

"Alright, then I guess that's settled." She swung her purse over her shoulder and looked down at Rosie, who was fast asleep in the chair by my desk.

"I'll carry her," I offered before Quinn could pick her up.

"You don't have to; I can get her."

"Like your brother said, quit being so stubborn."

Her brows rose, and her lips puckered into a look I had seen on my mom several times.

"And so it begins," she muttered.

We got back to my apartment a little after eight. I helped her get Rosie in bed and made sure the bathroom light was on before I shut the door and joined Quinn in the kitchen.

"I couldn't find much in your fridge, so I made you a peanut butter and jelly sandwich," she said, handing it to me wrapped in a paper towel.

"Thank you, but you didn't have to fix me anything to eat. I'll be sure to get some groceries tomorrow."

"You don't have to do that," she said before taking a bite of hers. "We're only here for one night."

I chewed and let my facial expressions do the talking.

"Roman, we can't just live with you. What if we don't figure out who this is for a while? Eventually, we'll need to go back to our apartment and get on with our lives."

"You'll stay as long as you need to, Quinn. It's not a big deal, and I actually like the company."

"You do?" The look she gave me said that she was calling my bluff.

"Yeah, it's kinda nice to have someone to talk to at night."

"I guess." She shrugged and pushed the last bite into her mouth. "It's been so long since I've had someone to talk to besides Rosie that I don't know if I even know how to have an adult conversation anymore."

"I'm sure it's been hard."

She walked to the sink and grabbed a glass out of the cabinet before filling it with water. She took a drink and then turned to me, holding the glass to her chest.

"I miss him."

"I'm sorry, I can't imagine losing someone like that."

I finished my sandwich and tossed the paper towel in the trash before grabbing a glass and filling it with water. We stood side by side in front of the sink, drinking our water, when she spoke again.

"I've been thinking about his accident tonight, and there's something that just never sat right with me about it."

"What's that?" I turned my head toward her.

"Justin was with three other agents in the car when they got in the accident, but he was the only one who didn't make it. They said that he had been fumbling with his seat belt and had taken it off for a moment when the car crashed. If he had been wearing it, he would have had some minor injuries, but he would likely still be here."

"Were the other agents injured in the accident?"

"Yeah, but only minor injuries. I think one guy broke his leg, and another had some fractured ribs, but nothing life-threatening. Justin was the only one who wasn't wearing a seat belt and was ejected through the window. He died on impact."

"God, Quinn," I sighed, not knowing what to say.

"What if his death wasn't an accident?" she asked, turning to face me as she set her water on the counter beside her.

"You don't think it was?"

She inhaled slowly and looked around before meeting my eyes.

"No, I think my husband was murdered."

Thirteen

Quinn

8 Days Ago

When I woke up, I felt lost and disoriented as I looked around, wondering why I felt so comfortable where I was. Then I remembered that I had slept at Roman's again and ended up cuddling his pillow most of the night because it smelled like him.

We stayed up talking for a few hours as I launched into my theory about how Justin hadn't just died in a car accident; he had been murdered. There was nothing that I could do to prove it, but it felt good to finally get the thoughts out of my head. Roman was kind enough to sit there and listen, even though I felt like a crazy person when the only thing I could come up with as to why Justin would never have taken his seat belt off in a moving car was because he was too *by the rules*.

But it was true—Justin never did anything that even slightly deviated into a gray area. He was, by nature, a goody-two-shoes, and everyone knew it. If you were planning to break any rules or skirt outside of what was considered ethical—you made sure he didn't find out about it because he would tell on you.

That was why it had been so weird to me when they told me that he had been ejected from the car because he had taken his seat belt off when the accident happened. I argued that he would never do that, and his partner had insisted that it was locked and uncomfortable, so he took it off to adjust it. While it was something that I would do—and had done several times—it wasn't something that he would do. Not even if the car was stopped at a red light. He would have waited until the car was safely parked somewhere before taking it off.

Roman had entertained my endless rambling on the subject until I got too tired to continue and called it a night. I hadn't bothered to apologize for intruding on his space again since it had been him who had insisted that we stay. Unfortunately, this time I didn't plan ahead, so I didn't have a change of clothes for Rosie or myself, and there was no way in hell that I was going to be late getting her to school again.

My alarm on my watch went off at five, so I rolled out of bed and shuffled down the hallway, hoping not to wake him. This time, I made sure to peek in the living room to make sure we didn't have another shower incident. I still couldn't get that beautiful sight out of my head—which I wasn't complaining about.

I snuck into the living room and smiled when I saw him still asleep on the couch. I turned and headed to the bathroom, feeling slightly anxious about leaving Rosie by herself until I remembered that Roman was here and no one was going to get into his apartment without him hearing them first.

I closed the bathroom door but didn't lock it in case Rosie woke up and was looking for me. The shower felt wonderful as I stood under the hot water and let it massage my tense muscles. I would love to fill the tub and just soak for a few hours, but I couldn't remember the last time I had done that.

Not wanting to use all of the hot water, I finished up and stepped out, wrapping a towel around my body. I looked for one to dry my hair with but didn't see any, so I tugged the one off of my body and quickly bent over to dry it as best I could so it wasn't soaking wet.

When I stood up, I gasped and tried to clutch the towel to my body before it fell to the floor. Standing before me was Roman, rubbing the sleep from his eyes before they focused on my naked body. He went from half asleep to wide awake in less than a second.

"Shit, I'm so sorry," he murmured, trying to look away. "I didn't think before I came in and didn't hear the shower. I thought you were still sleeping; it's early."

He bent down and handed me the towel while he looked away. I took it and wrapped it around myself as quickly as I could.

"I got up early because I need to swing by my place to get a change of clothes for Rosie and me before school, and she can't be late again."

"I really am sorry for walking in on you," he said, but there was something in his eyes that said he wasn't sorry at all.

"I guess we're almost even given that I walked in on you the other day."

I tried to laugh and make a joke out of it, but instead, it came out as some weird, muffled, strangled cry type of noise that I had never heard before in my life.

He smiled, and I looked away, suddenly feeling more embarrassed about it.

"Maybe not *even*," I muttered, thinking how I had only seen him from the waist up, whereas he had seen everything.

"Well, we'll try to make a schedule next time to keep this from happening again."

I could hear the laughter in his voice and clutched the towel tighter to my body. He stepped out and pulled the door behind him to give me some privacy to get dressed.

By the time I was done, Rosie was already awake and talking with Roman in the living room. I got our stuff ready while he jumped in the shower, then we ran by my apartment to change before rushing to school. Rosie didn't care about how quickly we had to walk since she had gotten a doughnut for breakfast when I didn't have time to stop for something healthier.

She walked into her classroom just as the final bell had rung. Her teachers gave us a quick wave before closing the door. I sighed a breath of relief that we had made it on time and leaned against the wall next to Roman. Unfortunately, there wasn't much time to linger in the hall and catch my breath if I wanted to get to work on time. If I kept showing up late, I would find myself in my boss's office again, listening to another lecture about punctuality and job responsibilities.

I pushed off the wall, and we started heading down the hallway when I felt Roman's hand brush against mine. The jolt of electricity that passed between us was enough to make my heart skip a beat, and suddenly I found myself anxious for the day to be over so I could go back to Roman's.

Fourteen

Roman

8 Days Ago

I waited until the end of the day to take my lunch so I could go to the grocery store and be back before Quinn and Rosie got there. I had picked Trevor's brain about what kind of foods kids liked to eat, but when neither of us had any idea, we found ourselves on some popular food blog with an abundance of options that looked easy and kid friendly.

I knew that Quinn was already struggling with the thought of staying with me for a while, so I wanted to make it as comfortable for them as possible. I picked up enough food to last us more than a few days and wondered how I was going to fit everything in the fridge, but that was a problem for another day.

Quinn and Rosie got there a little after six while I stirred the boiling pasta on the stove.

"You're cooking?" Quinn asked with a smile as she shut the door behind her. This morning I had given her the spare key even though she fought me on it. I had also volunteered to pick Rosie up and take her back to work with me until Quinn got home. She had refused and said that things needed to be as normal as possible for Rosie right now, which meant that Sandra would pick her up when she got out around one, and then Quinn would get her on her way home.

I hated not being there to watch over Rosie while she was with her grandma, but I also knew Sandra almost my entire life and trusted that she was safe there. Just because Sandra hadn't known about the van last time didn't mean she was incapable of protecting her granddaughter. She had grown up in a life of military and law enforcement officers, so it wasn't like she was clueless about what was going on. Mike had gotten her up to date, and Sandra was fully on board with everything that we were trying to do to protect Rosie.

"I cook," I laughed, grabbing the towel hanging over my shoulder. "Not often, but I still know what I'm doing." I opened the oven door and used the towel to take out the pan of chicken that I had baked. There were two chicken breasts that I had seasoned for Quinn and me, and then a third breast that I had cut into bite-sized pieces and breaded to make chicken nuggets for Rosie.

I set the pan on the back of the stove and turned the oven off. The pasta was done, so I removed it from the heat and drained it before adding it to the bowl of alfredo sauce that I had already warmed up.

"Go wash up while I help with dinner," Quinn said to Rosie, gently tousling her hair as she bounced off toward the bathroom.

A few seconds later, we heard the water turn on, and Rosie started singing Twinkle, Twinkle, Little Star.

"What can I help with?" Quinn asked, standing beside me at the stove.

I tried not to move, afraid that I would get burned if I did. It wasn't the heat from the stove that had me worried—it was the chemistry that was sizzling between us that scared me.

"I'm good," I answered, my voice thick and scratchy.

"You sure?"

She was close—too close—to where I could feel the tingle of goosebumps as her bare arm brushed against mine.

I nodded and muttered an *mmmhmm* before stepping away

to grab the plates from the cabinet. I turned around to set them down when I crashed into her again. This time it was her fingers that grabbed onto my body to hold me steady before they trailed across my ribs.

"Quinn," I breathed, still holding the plates but not bothering to move away from her touch.

"Yeah?" she asked, her fingers still making delicate trails around my abs.

"When you touch me like that…"

She lifted her eyes and looked into mine as a moment passed between us.

"You make it really hard not to throw these plates to the ground and kiss the hell out of you," I murmured, closing my eyes while trying to keep my grip on said plates.

Before she could respond, Rosie was heading down the hallway, singing another song. Quinn yanked her hands away and stepped back, tucking her head as she turned to the stove. I tried to ignore the way my dick was straining against my briefs but was thankful that my shirt and jeans were enough to hide it.

I put the plates on the counter and then grabbed some silverware while Quinn helped bring the food to the table. It wasn't a big table, but there was plenty of room for the three of us to sit and enjoy a meal together.

Rosie's eyes lit up when she saw her chicken nuggets, and I felt relieved that I hadn't screwed it up. I set a bowl of steamed broccoli and cauliflower on the table, assuming it would be for Quinn and myself, but I was pleasantly surprised when Rosie asked for some. I was impressed with how much she ate as she twirled noodles on her fork and giggled every time she made a slurping sound.

Quinn and I talked about random stuff at dinner, in between stories from Rosie about the things that happened at school or while she was with Sandra. Once we were done, Quinn offered to help clean up, but I insisted that she go get Rosie's bath started, and I would take care of it.

In addition to groceries, I had also grabbed a few things for them at the store that they would need here: shampoo, conditioner, toothbrushes, and of course, a bottle of bubble bath with princesses on it that smelled like strawberries. Rosie squealed when she saw it and asked Quinn if she could take the biggest bubble bath *ever* as she jumped up and down excitedly.

I had cooked extra for dinner, knowing that there would be enough for Quinn to take some to work for lunch. I wasn't sure if she usually packed a lunch, but I hadn't seen her take anything with her the few days I had gone with her to take Rosie to school. She didn't strike me as someone who ate out a lot, so I assumed she had been too busy and was likely skipping lunch while she tried to make up hours.

I didn't worry about leftovers for myself since tomorrow was Friday, and I was having lunch with Trevor and Max to get some updates on the items he was working on. It felt like it had already been a long time since we first talked about it when it had only been a few days. Life was suddenly chaotic, and I was having difficulty getting in the groove with things.

Rosie giggled from the bathroom, and I smiled, thankful to hear how happy and carefree she sounded. I hated that she lived in a world where bad things happened to sweet, innocent children like her, but I was determined to make sure that she never experienced it. Losing her father was tragic enough.

A little while later, Quinn came down the hall and plopped down on the couch beside me.

"I didn't think I was ever going to get her out of that bath," she laughed. "Thank you for picking up the bubble bath for her, that was really nice of you."

"Of course, not a problem. I also grabbed a few other things for you guys and left them on the counter."

"I saw, thank you for those as well. You don't have to keep buying us stuff and feeding us. I'm more than happy to help pay for stuff or bring our own—"

"Quinn, it's okay to let people help you," I said, interrupting her.

She sighed and sank lower on the couch.

"It's hard. I had so much help when Justin first died, which was great, but now I feel like I should be able to handle things on my own. It's been four years. I shouldn't need anyone anymore."

"It doesn't matter how long it's been. It's okay to need help still. That doesn't make you weak or any less of a mother."

"I don't know how single mothers do it with more than one kid," she laughed, resting her head on the cushion. "I only have one, and it feels like I'm always in over my head and drowning."

"They do exactly what you're doing—they just keep pushing forward, one step at a time."

Her phone rang, and she pulled it out of her pocket, smiling as she looked at the caller ID before answering.

"Hey, Mama."

I thought about getting up to give her some privacy for her phone call, but I got a text message from Max before I could.

Max: Is she with you tonight?

Me: Yes, they're both here now.

Max: Keep them there and make sure your doors are locked.

Me: What happened?

Max: Someone broke into her apartment. It'll be a few days before she can go back.

Me: Did they take anything valuable?

Max: It's more so what they left.

Another text message came through, but this time it was a picture of a seat belt lying on Quinn's bed.

I was still staring at my phone when Quinn ended her call and was staring at me.

"Everything okay?" she asked.

"Yeah," I lied, tucking my phone into my pocket. "You?"

"That was my mom asking if she can keep Rosie tomorrow after school for a sleepover since it's Friday and we don't have plans on Saturday."

"That's sweet of her; I'm sure she would enjoy that."

"Do you think it's okay to let her stay?"

"I don't see why not," I shrugged. "But if you're uncomfortable about it, you can always say no."

"I already told her yes, so I would feel bad backing out now. Besides, we don't even know if anyone is still watching her. I haven't noticed anything weird, have you?"

I wanted to tell her about the picture Max had just sent me but decided that it was better to wait until I could talk to him. I pulled my phone back out of my pocket and sent him a quick text, asking if anyone was going to call and tell Quinn about the break-in.

"I haven't noticed anything," I replied, putting my phone

on the couch beside me. "But that doesn't mean that we can stop being vigilant. We have to keep our guard up and make sure we know where Rosie is at all times."

She chewed her nail and thought about it. Before she could say anything else, her phone rang again.

"Sorry, it's Mike this time."

She answered, and I knew he was calling to tell her about the apartment.

"Oh my God," she whispered, holding her hand to her chest. "Okay, yeah, I understand."

I hated the look of fear in her eyes right now.

"I'll see if I can stay with Roman for a few more days," she said as she caught me nodding my head. It wasn't even a question of whether she *could* stay with me. I would make sure that they did, especially now that someone had been in their apartment.

Rosie came into the living room after getting her pajamas on and her teeth brushed. Quinn finished up with her phone call and seemed flustered.

"What's wrong, Mama?" Rosie asked, curling up beside her on the couch.

"Nothing, sweet girl." She gently brushed her fingers across Rosie's forehead, making her eyes flutter as she tried to stay awake.

"I can go by your apartment to grab some clothes and stuff if you want?" I offered, knowing that it was another thing weighing heavily on her mind.

"It's okay, I can try to go in the morning."

"Quinn."

She rolled her eyes and exhaled.

"You wouldn't know what to pack," she objected.

"You can tell me. I am pretty smart, you know. I ran some pretty intense operations in the Marines; I think I can handle packing up some stuff."

"You really want to go through my personal belongings and pick the bras and panties that I'm going to wear for a few days?"

I knew that she was being sarcastic, but there was actually nothing that I wanted more. Although, the thought of her wearing them for me was even more thrilling. Heat spread quickly throughout my body, adding a touch of color to my naturally tanned cheeks.

"What if you had an escort?" I raised a brow, challenging her while also trying to steer the conversation in another direction.

"An escort?"

I nodded.

"Like Mike?"

"I can't think of anyone better."

She tilted her head back, closed her eyes, and groaned.

"Ugh. Fine."

"Do you want to go tonight or tomorrow morning?"

She thought about it for a minute before picking up her phone and rolling her eyes again.

"I'll see if he can go with me tonight; that way we don't have to rush as much in the morning."

I leaned back and smiled, feeling slightly satisfied that she wasn't fighting me on it.

Fifteen

Roman

7 Days Ago

I spent most of the morning in an upbeat, happy mood as I counted down the hours until Quinn would be off work and heading back to my apartment. I knew that it was foolish to think that anything could—or would—happen between us, but I still couldn't fight the grin that felt plastered to my face since I woke up. Not having Rosie with us tonight would allow us the time to talk and not have to worry about what she might overhear.

By ten, Trevor came bouncing into the office, a smile bigger than mine spread across his cheeks. I pushed away from my desk and swiveled my chair to face him.

"I don't think I've seen you this happy about it being Friday since you had tickets to take Elena to her first Yankees game."

"Well, this is soooo much better than a Yankees game," he said, sliding into the chair behind his desk.

I gasped and held a hand to my heart, pretending to be stunned by this information.

"*What* could possibly be better than the Yankees?"

"Elena agreed that we can start trying to have a baby after Max's wedding. She's finally ready!"

"That's awesome, man! Happy humping!"

His grin stretched across his face as our phones dinged

at the same time with a text message alert. I had almost expected it to be from Max about lunch today since we both got messages, but mine was from Quinn.

My fingers rushed to open the message to read it.

Quinn: My mom wants to pick Rosie up from school today.

Me: That's nice of her. I'm sure she'll enjoy spending time with your mom.

Quinn: I'm worried someone will be watching them like last time.

Me: That's always a possibility, but it would be with whoever picked her up.

Quinn: Should I pick her up instead?

Me: If it makes you feel better, I don't see why not.

Me: Do you want me to meet you there?

Quinn: You don't have to do that but thank you.

Me: I don't mind.

Quinn: Hold on

I set my phone down and waited for her next message.

I lifted my head and found Trevor staring at his phone, a cheesy grin plastered to his face again. He looked up and saw me watching him with a brow raised.

"Elena is already thinking of baby names," he answered as his fingers flew across his phone.

"And here you thought she wasn't ready," I laughed.

"Hey, what can I say? I'm not used to good things happening this easily."

"I think you've more than paid your dues, my brother. Only the best things are heading your way from here on out."

I knew how much he wanted to be a father and was glad that things looked like they were finally heading in that direction for him. Elena was young—ten years younger than him—and that had put them on different pages about starting a family for a few months now.

He smiled and let his shoulders relax.

"Thanks, man."

I returned his smile and then picked up my phone to check the new message from Quinn.

Quinn: Mike is going with her to pick Rosie up, which works better since my boss just called another mandatory meeting.

Me: See, everything always works out. She'll be more than safe with Mike and your mom there.

Quinn: Apparently Mike is also staying the night at my mom's house. I think something has him worried.

Me: I don't know any more than you do, but I imagine that the break-in last night has him on heightened alert like it does us.

Quinn: Yeah, I guess. I just feel like there's more that he's not telling me.

Me: I wouldn't worry about it. Mike wouldn't do anything to put you or Rosie in danger.

Quinn: True.

Me: Try not to obsess over it. The weekend will officially be here before you know it.

Quinn: I wanted to talk to you about that.

Me: The weekend?

Quinn: Yes. I don't want you to feel like you have to babysit me tonight while Rosie is at my mom's house. I can find something to do so I'm not in your hair.

Me: I don't have plans, and you're not in my hair.

Quinn: I don't want to impose.

Me: Stop.

Quinn: …….

Me: Whatever you're typing—just delete it.

Me: I need to get back to work but think about what you want for dinner, and I'll pick up something on my way home.

Quinn: You're so bossy.

Me: You like it.

Quinn: ……

Quinn: ……

Quinn: ……

I felt my insides flip as I waited for her to decide on whatever she was going to send. The dots would appear and then disappear for a few minutes before she finally pressed send.

Quinn: I'll check in with you at 4:30. Have a good day.

Me: You too.

I slid my phone to the side and tried to force myself to focus on work and not the endless thoughts on what Quinn might have been saying before she chickened out. *Did she like that I was bossy? Was it off-putting to her?* At the end of the day, we would be having our first dinner together by ourselves, and that felt like it meant more than it should.

Sixteen

Quinn

7 Days Ago

"What?" I laughed, pulling the greasy chili cheese dogs out of the to-go bag and setting them on the counter. "This is what I wanted for dinner."

"You never cease to surprise me," Roman laughed, his arm brushing against mine as he set the paper plates down.

"I try to eat healthy with Rosie, but every now and then, I just crave these chili dogs. That's how my butt got so big when I was pregnant with her. I think they actually put my picture on the wall at one point as their top customer because I went there so frequently and spent so much money on chili dogs. Justin never complained, not once. Not even when my ass grew two sizes," I snorted. "It never went away either," I commented, looking over my shoulder at my plump behind.

I watched Roman's eyes as they followed mine, landing on my ass before he sucked in a breath and looked away.

As much as I wanted to deny that things *didn't* feel different without Rosie here, I couldn't. It was like there was all of this sexual tension between us, crackling like electricity whenever we got close enough to each other for our bodies to touch.

"So, how many do you want?" Roman asked, studying the pile in front of us.

"I'll start with two and some fries."

"Start with? You're not playing, are you?"

"Nope," I replied, letting the *p* pop.

He smiled and shook his head as he piled two chili cheese dogs and some fries on a plate and handed it to me. We went to the living room and sat down on the couch, leaving the middle cushion empty between us.

We didn't bother with small talk as we ate. The food was too delicious to waste time with anything but eating it.

Roman took his first bite and closed his eyes as he chewed, a small moan escaping his lips. I tried to look away, but there was something so sexy about the way he looked that I couldn't help but imagine him eating something else.

I held the chili dog in front of my mouth, taking bites without paying attention while I continued to watch the show. His eyes were now open, but he still hadn't noticed me staring at him as he took another bite. I pushed the hotdog into my mouth, not realizing how far back I had shoved it until it hit the back of my throat, and I started choking.

I immediately pulled it out and started coughing as he dropped his to his plate and reached over to grab my bottle of water.

"Are you okay?" he asked as he handed it to me.

I nodded and took a drink, trying desperately to stop the coughing. It was so embarrassing, and how was I supposed to explain what happened? *I got so turned on watching you eat your chili dog that I tried to deep throat mine.*

"I'm okay," I managed to get out before taking another drink. "I was just a little distracted."

He arched a brow and leaned back against the couch, a faint smirk appearing on his face as if he knew exactly what I had been distracted by.

"Wieners do that sometimes," he replied nonchalantly as he stuck his tongue in his cheek.

My cheeks felt like they were on fire as the heat rushed over them.

"I wouldn't know," I said shyly, looking away as I chugged the rest of my water.

A look flashed across his face, but I ignored it as I got up and collected my plate.

"Are you done?" I asked, nodding to his.

"Yeah, I'll take it though."

"I don't mind." I pushed my hand toward him for him to put his plate on mine. Instead, he grabbed my plate from me and stood up, invading my space, and taking up all of the clean air around me.

"I do. Sit down and relax. I'll clean up."

I knew better than to fight him on cleaning up my trash and sat down.

"Do you want another bottle of water? I also have milk, and I think I might have a few beers."

"Water is good, thank you."

He shuffled around in the kitchen as he threw away our plates, then joined me on the couch again.

"Here you go," he said as he handed me the cold bottle of water.

"Thank you."

I debated rubbing it across my body to try to take some of the heat away, then realized that it would be even more sexual than my near-death by wiener a few minutes ago.

"Do you want to watch a movie?" Roman offered, clearing the awkward silence between us.

"Sure." I smiled and felt some of the tension start to dissipate when he smiled back at me.

He scrolled through the channels, trying to find something, but neither of us was that motivated to pick something. Finally, he gave up and left it on *Die Hard*.

I tried to focus on the movie, but my mind was constantly distracted, wondering how Rosie was doing and whether she was having fun. When I wasn't obsessing over her, I was thinking about my apartment and the seat belt that was left on my bed. Someone was trying to send me a message—that much was clear. I just wish I knew who it was and what they wanted.

I was so lost in thought that I hadn't heard Roman speak. My legs were extended in front of me, taking up the space on the cushion that was supposed to be separating us. Instead, my toes were pressed firmly against his thick thigh, and his hand rested on my ankle.

"I'm sorry, what?" I asked, feeling bad for missing what he said.

"I asked if you wanted another bottle of water," he said softly.

I looked down at the one in my hand, now empty after slowly chugging it without paying attention.

"I'm good, thank you. Soon I'll be swimming around here with all of the water I've drunk."

"I have plenty," he laughed.

I felt my lips curl up into a grin.

"What's on your mind?" he asked as he gently squeezed my foot.

"Everything," I laughed, though it wasn't a lie.

"Wanna talk about it?"

"Not really," I shook my head. "For once, I just want a break where I don't have to think about anything or worry about anyone but myself. I know that's selfish, but I can't remember when the last time was that I was able to just be me. Not a wife. Not a mother. Not an agent. Just me."

I leaned back further into the couch and sighed heavily.

"It's not selfish," he replied quietly, pulling my foot up onto his lap as he massaged it. "It's okay to take time for yourself, and it's also okay to let someone else take care of you."

I eyed him suspiciously, waiting for there to be some sort of *but* added to it. *Moms don't get breaks; that's the job you signed up for. Wives need to learn how to balance work and family life; it's up to them to make those ends meet without anyone noticing their struggle. Women don't ask for help; we make do with what we have.*

I shook my head to clear the thoughts that I had allowed my brain to ingrain into my memory over the years. Justin was a good man, but even he had flaws—and those flaws were with how he viewed women and their role in the marriage.

"I honestly wouldn't have any idea what that's like. I moved out the day after I turned eighteen, and I've been on my own since then."

"It's never too late to start."

He kept working my tired, sore feet, rotating between them as his strong hands massaged every inch. Now that Rosie was getting older, I had started taking her for mommy and daughter dates to get pedicures, but even those massages were nothing compared to what Roman was doing.

"How are you still single?" I blurted out, watching him carefully.

He smiled but didn't look up. His fingers pressed against the pad of my foot, putting enough pressure to release some of the tension that had built up.

"I haven't met the right woman."

"Are you looking?"

"I'd like to think that I would know when I found her," he shrugged, gently dropping my foot, and finally looking up at me. "But as we both know, life doesn't always work out that way. Sometimes the things we want are the things that we can't have."

My heart fluttered at his words, and I couldn't help but wonder if he was talking about us. I could see something hidden in his eyes when he said it—an almost sadness.

"What do you want?" I asked bravely.

He swallowed hard, looking around the room before turning back to me.

"You."

Seventeen

Roman

7 Days Ago

My words hung heavily in the air between us. Did I expect to say that to Quinn? No. Did I regret admitting it to her? Also no.

Her body was rigid next to mine, her feet pulled back to her side of the couch, making the distance between us feel like it was more than it was. I missed touching her already but knew that I didn't have the right to, to begin with.

"Are you joking with me?" she asked quietly, barely above a whisper.

I squared my shoulders and rolled my head back on my neck, looking ahead of me instead of at her.

"I would never joke about something like that."

She adjusted on the couch beside me, pulling one of the throw pillows up to her chest as she held it against her.

"But I'm sorry if I made you uncomfortable. That was never my intention, and you have my word that you're safe here with me. Just because I have feelings for you doesn't mean I'll act on them."

I glanced at her and found her watching me as she rubbed her fingers across her mouth.

Not wanting to make her feel awkward or uneasy, I got up and went into the kitchen. I had no idea what I was going to do in there, but at least it would give me a few minutes to think without having Quinn near me. It was almost like she was a siren, calling to me and luring me into a murky area that I had no business being.

I was working on cleaning the coffee pot out and getting it programmed to run in the morning when I heard Quinn come in. I kept my back to her, too nervous to face her just yet. I knew I had to at some point, but I had put my big foot in my mouth and now had to pay the price for that.

She moved around behind me, doing something at the sink. I turned to grab the coffee from the cabinet when she turned around, and we collided again. I wanted to make a joke about how we couldn't keep meeting this way, but it didn't feel like it was as light as it should be. *Maybe there was a reason we kept running into each other. Maybe it was the universe trying to push us together.*

"Sorry," she laughed nervously. Her thick lashes fluttered as she kept her eyes down, afraid to look up at me.

My hands instinctively reached out and held onto her hips. She didn't move away and slowly, her hands slid up my arms and held onto me as if she was afraid to let go. Her chest rose and fell heavily, the air between us thick with desire we both felt.

She looked up, her blue eyes gazing into mine.

I knew that I needed to pull away and let her go, but I couldn't.

My fingers dug deeper into her hips, claiming her as mine.

Her lips parted slightly as I leaned toward her, unable to stop myself. My lips gently brushed against hers, the electricity of it enough to permanently brand this moment into my memory forever.

She lifted her hands and wrapped them around my neck, pulling me closer as she kissed me back, teasing my lips with the tip of her tongue as it begged for access.

I groaned and kissed her deeper, our tongues dancing to a song they'd heard a million times. Her nails scratched at my skin as I lifted her by the waist, and she wrapped her legs around me. I walked to the counter and set her on it as our mouths devoured each other with a carnal need I had never felt before.

Quinn pulled away for a split second, completely breathless. Her chest heaved as she swiped a finger across her bottom lip, swollen from my teeth gently nipping at it.

"I'm sorry," I breathed, resting my forehead against hers.

"I'm not," she answered before lifting my chin with her finger.

She looked into my eyes, and I could see that she meant it. She wanted this to happen as much as I did.

"We shouldn't be doing this," I muttered, frustrated with myself for not being able to stop.

"It's wrong," she agreed, lifting my shirt up and over my head. Once it was off, she threw it to the side and leaned in to plant kisses along my chest. "So wrong."

"Quinn," I whispered her name, closing my eyes as I took in how fucking amazing it felt to have her soft lips pressed against my body. My dick twitched in anticipation, and I almost groaned in response.

"Let's just live in the moment, Roman. Just once."

There were so many things rushing through my brain that I should have been focused on, but the only thing that registered at that moment was the way my name sounded rolling off of her tongue.

"Please," she begged. "I don't want to overthink this. I just want one night where I get to feel like this."

She continued kissing her way across my stomach as her fingers unfastened my belt and started pulling the zipper down.

"Feel like what, Quinn? Tell me."

She lazily trailed her tongue up my body, pausing briefly to give me one-word answers.

"Wanted."

"Sexy."

She flicked my nipple with her tongue before continuing.

"Free."

"Desired."

"You're all of those things, Quinn," I answered as I held the back of her head while she worked her way back down my torso. "You're all of that and so much more."

She pulled my zipper the rest of the way down and gently reached in, rubbing my throbbing cock with the palm of her hand.

"I knew you'd be big," she said, giving it a firm squeeze.

Before I could answer, her phone started ringing.

Her fingers pushed into the opening of my briefs, ready to pull my dick out when it rang again.

"Your phone is ringing," I said through gritted teeth, not wanting this to stop.

Suddenly she stopped and let go, her eyes widening when she realized that it could be someone calling about Rosie. I scooted back and helped her down from the counter as she ran over to grab her phone while I adjusted myself.

"Hey, Mom," she said heavily into the phone.

I stayed in the kitchen, giving her space while I tried

to compose myself. Quinn talked to her mom for a few minutes before Rosie got on the line to tell her goodnight. I leaned against the fridge and scrubbed a hand down my face while I thought about what had just happened.

My phone buzzed in my pocket with a text message.

Mike: How's everything going over there?

I swallowed hard, wondering how I would look him in the eye the next time I saw him. He would be pissed if he knew what Quinn and I had done. Thankfully it didn't go any further, but still, I didn't imagine that he would be pleased knowing that his little sister had been rubbing my dick and licking her way across my chest.

Me: We're good.

There—short and simple. That wouldn't give anything away because our texts to each other were always quick anyway.

Mike: Call if you need anything.

There were plenty of things that I needed but nothing that I would ask him for. Quinn, on the other hand…

Eighteen

Quinn

6 Days Ago

Roman and I had called it a night early last night after almost going at it like horny teenagers on his kitchen counter. I had no idea what had come over me, but something about the chemistry between us was so intoxicating that I couldn't stop myself. I wanted more. *Needed more.*

I couldn't remember the last time I had been touched like that, and the funny thing was that he barely even touched me. But the way his fingers dug into my hips was such a turn-on, almost as if he was afraid to let me go. And that kiss—man, that kiss had nearly taken my breath away. No one had ever kissed me with so much passion and desire, not even Justin.

We had gone our separate ways—me to the bedroom and him to the couch—but I knew he hadn't gone to sleep until well after midnight, just like I hadn't. Instead, I had sat on the bed, running my fingers over my lips, and remembering the way his had felt against mine. I was daydreaming of the next time I could kiss him when it occurred to me that there might not be a next time.

Roman had admitted that he wanted me, but that didn't mean anything. He also admitted that he wouldn't act on it, which was why I had initiated everything. But what if he really didn't want anything beyond what we already did? Hell—I wasn't sure if he had even wanted that to happen or if he was just lost in the moment like I was. His rock-hard dick was on board, even if his heart and mind hadn't been made up yet.

I thought about Justin and found myself comparing them, which immediately made me feel guilty. Justin was my husband—the person that I had vowed to spend the rest of my life with—yet here I was, comparing all of his flaws to where Roman already excelled.

Justin had been a lazy lover, never bothering with foreplay unless it was my birthday or a holiday. We didn't have sex as often as I would have liked, and sometimes I wondered how I ever got pregnant with Rosie. I liked to believe that she was the miracle that I needed in my life and that God gave me that sweet baby to help fill some of the void and loneliness that I felt in my marriage.

But Roman—Roman was different. He was caring and attentive, constantly checking to make sure I was okay and doing little things to make life easier for me. From letting us stay with him to buying groceries for us, he had already gone above and beyond to ensure that we had the things we needed. He didn't disregard my feelings or brush me off when I was upset about something. That alone gave me this hope that was blossoming quicker than I could process it. *What would it be like to be with a guy like Roman?*

I had gotten up before the sun this morning and climbed out of bed, hoping to sneak in a shower without waking him up. From what I could tell, he was still asleep on the couch, so I cranked up the hot water and stood underneath it for a few minutes, letting it wash away all of the stress that had been building up.

When I was done, I wrapped a towel around my body and quickly dried my hair with the extra one that Rosie had been using. I looked around for my clean clothes, only to realize that I had left them on the bed.

I quietly opened the door and headed for the bedroom when I heard footsteps behind me. I turned around, expecting to see Roman.

Instead, I found Mike with a scowl set hard on his face as he looked me up and down.

"Is that what you're wearing around Roman?" he asked.

"No," I quickly shook my head and pulled the towel tighter around my body. "I forgot my clothes on the bed."

He nodded but didn't say anything.

"Why are you here this early?" I asked, suddenly irritated with him.

Just then, Roman appeared behind him, his face tight with anger.

"What's going on? What happened?" My heart started racing as I waited for them to tell me.

Finally, Mike sighed heavily and then looked me in the eyes.

"Rosie is missing."

Nineteen

Roman

6 Days Ago

"Rosie!" I called, checking the shrubs between Sandra's house and the neighbors. We had been looking for her for over thirty minutes, and no one had any idea where she had gone.

Sandra had woken up shortly after six and went to check on Rosie. When she found that she wasn't in her bed, she went to the living room and expected to find her with Mike, but she wasn't there either. Mike hadn't heard anything, and all of the doors and windows were still locked.

Their sister, Sonia had rushed over to help Sandra look for her while Mike went to my apartment to see if Rosie had gone there looking for Quinn. When she wasn't there, we all went back to Sandra's to continue the search while Sandra called the police to report a missing child. We all knew that they wouldn't do anything this early on, so I had reached out to Trevor and Max and asked for their help as well.

Quinn was walking the neighborhood with me while Mike checked the front and backyard of the house. Sonia and Sandra were searching inside the house, looking into every place that she might be able to hide.

I saw Max and Trevor heading our way and gave them a quick nod before walking up to knock on another neighbor's door. So far, I had been met with a few disgruntled growls for waking people up this early on a Saturday morning, but I couldn't care less. Rosie was missing, and I would stop at nothing to find her.

Quinn finished up at the house she was at, then met me on the street. Trevor and Max joined us a few minutes later.

"Any updates?" Max asked.

I shook my head and glanced at Quinn. Tears filled her eyes, and I could see that she was trying to keep it together and not fall apart.

"We're going to find her, I promise," Max assured her and gently squeezed her shoulder.

She sucked in a shaky deep breath and tried to let it out slowly.

"When was the last time anyone saw her?" Trevor asked, looking between Quinn and me.

"My mom said they went to bed around ten and that she was still in bed when my mom checked on her around midnight when she got up to use the restroom. Mike was up around four and confirmed that she was still in bed. So I guess a little over three hours ago."

Max's jaw clenched, and I knew what he was thinking. If someone took her, they were already long gone by now. Three hours was plenty of time for them to be in a different state, and we had absolutely no idea what direction they went.

"What do we do now?" she asked Max, a look of desperation on her face.

"We need to call this in, but if I know Mike, he already has. I'll check with him, and then we'll go from there. We'll get all hands on deck and move as quickly as possible."

Quinn turned and covered her face as the tears started to fall. I reached out to hug her, noticing the way Trevor was looking at me. I didn't care if he could see how I felt about her, I needed to be there for her and make sure she was okay.

I wrapped her in my arms and pulled her into my chest, allowing her a safe place to cry without everyone seeing. She wrapped my shirt in her hands and trembled as she cried.

I held her for what felt like forever, knowing that every second mattered but not being able to pull away. Max had already found Mike, and they were discussing who had already been contacted when I looked up and saw Rosie running down the street toward us with a woman walking behind her.

"Quinn, she's here," I said, turning her around.

"Rosie!" She took off running and grabbed her, holding her to her chest as tight as possible.

"We found her," I yelled to Max and Mike, who were standing on the porch. In a matter of seconds, everyone was out of the house and rushing out to see her.

"I'm so glad you're safe," Quinn cooed, still holding Rosie against her.

The woman approached us, smiling at the mother and daughter that had been reunited.

Quinn suddenly spotted the woman and set Rosie down, pushing her behind her. I stepped forward and picked Rosie up, ensuring she wasn't going anywhere.

"What the hell are you doing with my daughter?" Quinn spat out through gritted teeth. Her fists were clenched at her sides.

"Woah, woah, woah," Mike said, quickly stepping in and putting some space between Quinn and the woman before she could punch her.

"Move out of the way," Quinn demanded, trying to push past him.

"I'm not here to cause any trouble," the woman said with her hands in the air. "I was simply trying to bring her home."

"Bullshit." Quinn's nostrils flared, and I wondered if I should take Rosie inside so she didn't have to see any of this.

"I know that we've had our issues Quinn, but I really was just trying to help."

"Why don't you tell us what happened and why you had my niece," Mike said, one arm still extended to hold Quinn back.

"I was waiting for the train and spotted her. But, I didn't see Quinn with her and started to worry."

"Who was she with?" I asked.

"I don't know. It looked like a woman, but they had a hoodie covering their face, so I couldn't get a good look." She looked at Rosie and smiled sadly. "I knew that she didn't know them and that I needed to step in and make sure she got home okay."

"Thank you," Mike said softly.

"It's the least I could do given everything that happened." She lowered her head and walked away.

"That's it? You're just going to let her go?" I asked Mike, trying to keep the anger in my voice from startling Rosie.

"Don't worry, I know who she is and where to find her. Let's get Rosie inside and see if we can figure out what happened," he said, reaching for his niece. She wrapped her arms around his neck and let him carry her into the house.

I waited outside with Quinn for a few minutes while she did whatever she needed to do to calm herself down.

"Okay, so who was that woman?" I asked as we headed inside.

"She worked with Justin and was the one driving the car when he was killed."

Twenty

Quinn

6 Days Ago

"Alright, Rosie, can you tell us what happened and why you left grandma's house?" I asked as I sat on the coffee table in front of the couch and studied her.

We had all taken turns looking her over to make sure she didn't have any injuries, but that didn't keep me calm, knowing that she had been away from us for who knows how long, with someone that we didn't know.

"I heard a puppy crying, so I got up and looked out the window. I couldn't see anything, but it kept crying louder. I knew that it needed help, so I went to the kitchen and checked to see if it was stuck in the dog door."

"Was there a dog stuck in it?" I sat up straight and tried to keep the stress from showing on my face.

"No, but I could see a puppy, so I stuck my head in and tried to find where it went. It was still crying, so I climbed through and looked for it in the backyard."

"Then what happened?"

"There was a woman by the street looking for her dog. She said that she was walking it and it got scared and ran away."

"Do you remember what she looked like?"

She shook her head.

"Did she ask you for anything?"

She nodded.

"What did she say?"

"She said that she needed my help finding her dog and that she would make sure we didn't go too far from the house so my grandma didn't get scared if she couldn't find me."

I swallowed hard as I tucked that little nugget of information aside.

"Where did you guys go?"

"We stayed on the street, but then she thought she heard the dog crying further ahead, so we went that way looking for it."

"And then you guys ended up at the subway?"

"Yeah, she thought she saw the dog run down the stairs, so we followed after it."

I closed my eyes and took a moment to compose myself before talking to her about what had happened.

I felt my mom squeeze my knee reassuringly.

"I did something wrong, didn't I?" Rosie asked, looking at me with tears in her eyes.

I was at a loss for words, struggling to explain to her the danger that she was in. I didn't want to traumatize her, but I also knew that she needed to know the truth in order to protect herself.

"You didn't do anything wrong, but we need to talk about what happened," Mike said, sitting down beside me. I scooted over to make room for him.

"I know that you wanted to help that woman find her dog because you are such a helpful little girl, but unfortunately, she was using the lost dog as an excuse to get you to leave the house."

"Why would she do that?"

"Do you remember in school when you guys learned about strangers and how you shouldn't talk to them or go with someone if you don't know them?" I asked, finally feeling the strength to have this conversation with her.

She nodded, and her face fell when she realized what she had done.

"I was worried about the puppy."

"I know, baby."

"Did she want to kidnap me?" Rosie whispered.

I nodded and felt the tears burn my skin as they trickled down my face.

"What was she going to do with me?"

"I don't know, my love. But please promise me that you won't ever go with someone you don't know, ever again."

"I promise, Mama." She jumped up from the couch and landed on my lap with her arms wrapped around my neck.

"I'm sorry, I didn't mean to scare everyone."

"I know," I sighed, holding her tightly against me. "I promise that I won't ever let anything happen to you. I love you so much."

"I love you too, Mama."

We hugged for a few minutes until she finally pulled away and asked to use the restroom. My mom went with her, all of us afraid to let her out of our sight.

Once they were out of the room, I sat on the couch and

pulled a pillow onto my lap.

"You okay?" Roman asked.

I shook my head and let the tears fall, not caring that I was still surrounded by my brother, Trevor, and Max. Sonia was busy working on taking the dog door out, and her boyfriend was on his way over with supplies to help her.

"Why is this happening to her?" I sobbed, wiping my face with the back of my hands.

"I don't know, but we're going to figure it out," Mike assured me.

"I agree—we'll find whoever it is before they get another chance to take her," Max added.

"They almost had her. If Julia hadn't been there this morning, who knows where Rosie would be right now. They got her out of the house without any of us knowing. And even worse—they knew personal details about the house. Like how would they know to lure her to the dog door if they hadn't been here before? Mom hasn't had a dog in two years. And you all heard what Rosie said about the woman knowing she was at her grandma's house." My voice was rising as my panic started to set in.

"The nice thing is that they're consistent," Max said from where he was leaning against the wall. "They want us to know they have a personal connection to you guys. They've left signs along the way. That makes it easier to narrow it down because it's not a random attack."

"What do you think the coincidence is that Julia just happened to be at the right place at the right time?" Trevor asked.

I hadn't even thought of that until now, but he had a good point.

"She also knew to bring her back to my mom's house—not our apartment. We live in the same one that Justin lived in, so it's not like she wouldn't know where it was. Lord knows she was there often enough when they worked together."

"Do you think that she was the one who took Rosie?" Roman inquired from the other side of the couch. "Maybe she was the one who lured her away and then brought her back? It could be a game for her to point out how easy it was to take her in the first place."

"It's possible, but if it was her, why not just take her and run? Why bring her back?" I chewed my nail anxiously.

A few minutes later, Rosie returned with my mom and curled up on the couch with me.

"Hey, Rosie?" I asked.

She tilted her head up and looked at me.

"Was the woman who was looking for her puppy the same woman that brought you back?"

She didn't have to think about it before she confidently shook her head.

"No, but she was really mad at the lady who lost her dog. They had a fight before she grabbed me and brought me home."

"What was the fight about?" I pushed, hoping she would remember in as much detail as she did about what color socks her best friend wore every day at school.

"I don't know, but they were whispering—but like mad whispers—and she told her, 'it's not time, what are you doing? You're going to mess everything up!' Then she grabbed my arm and brought me home."

I felt all eyes in the room on me and knew that we had a bigger problem than we could have ever imagined.

Twenty-One

Roman

5 Days Ago

"Okay, so where do we go from here?" I asked as I looked around my apartment at Mike, Trevor, and Max. Quinn and Rosie had stayed the night with me last night but left to spend the day at her mom's house while us guys tried to figure out a plan to keep Rosie safe.

"It's hard to say," Mike replied with a hint of frustration in his voice as he ran a hand through his hair.

"We know that it's not just one person that's involved," Max added. "There are several people at play, and that will make it even harder to narrow it down."

"There's also a strong FBI thread," Trevor said with a nod in Mike's direction.

"I know," he muttered. "I fucking hate this. I can't even go to my own team for help because I don't know who I can trust. We know Rosie is the ultimate target, but Quinn and I are also targets."

"Let's start at the beginning." Max stood up and paced the space between the kitchen and living room. "Things started when Rosie's teachers spotted a van across the street. They were the ones who said that she was being targeted. The police were called, but nothing happened because he was gone by the time they got there. After that, Quinn spotted the same van parked outside of her mom's house after she picked Rosie up from school when Quinn had a last-minute meeting at work—right?"

"Yeah, that's correct," I confirmed.

"And the person driving the van was wearing Mike's baseball cap that was stolen from his office?"

"Correct again," Mike said. "Very few people have access to my office, so it leads me to believe that someone in my department took it."

"Do you think that it was the same person wearing it and driving the van?"

Mike shrugged in response to Max's question.

"In addition to that, we know that Justin was killed on the job in a car accident and that he was the only one ejected from the vehicle because he wasn't wearing a seat belt. Were you with him when it happened?"

I looked over at Mike and noticed his jaw clenching as he balled his fists.

"No. I wasn't with him when it happened. We worked on two different cases, so we didn't cross paths much. Given that we were considered family, the department kept us separated and prohibited us from working on the same case."

"Do you know who all was in the car with him?" Max asked, folding his arms over his chest.

"From what I remember, it was Justin, Saul, Frank, and Julia."

"The woman from this morning," I confirmed. "Quinn told me that she was the one who was driving the car."

"Does she still work in witness protection?" Max turned to Mike.

"Yeah. She's still there."

"So she would have had access to your office?"

Mike nodded.

"And she knew about the car accident."

"You think she's responsible for all of this?" I asked Max, taking some of the pressure off of Mike.

"I think she's definitely involved. Between the seat belt left on Quinn's bed and the situation yesterday with Julia bringing Rosie home, it doesn't sit well with me. She's up to something, but I don't think she's working alone."

I turned to face Mike.

"Didn't you say that the last case that Justin was working on was a child trafficking case?"

"Yeah."

"How soon after the trial ended was Justin's accident?"

Mike closed his eyes and leaned his head back against the cushion.

"It was the same day."

"And the girl that was being protected was recently found dead, right?" I knew there was too much excitement in my voice, but I felt like we were finally cracking through this mystery and getting closer to knowing what was going on.

"About a week ago," Mike confirmed.

"And the guy she put away?" Max asked, sensing where I was going with this.

"There were two," Mike responded, pulling his phone out and typing something in the internet search bar. "A father and son. The father was the ringleader of the operation and got a life sentence."

"But the son?" Trevor asked.

"He was released two weeks ago."

Twenty-Two

Quinn

5 Days Ago

"Elias Salvador, son of Juan Salvador, age thirty-two, served five years for possession and distribution of child pornography."

I sat at the kitchen table at my mom's house and reached for the mugshot that Mike slid across the table to me.

"Before Justin died, he helped Ariel Wyland put the man who tortured and held her captive for ten years behind bars. Not only did they take down the ringleader of the operation, but they also caught his son, Elias as well. Unfortunately, there wasn't enough to hold him longer than five years, and as you already know, he's been granted early release and forced to register as a sex offender."

"You think this is who is watching Rosie?" I asked quietly.

My mom and Rosie were hanging out in my mom's bedroom, watching movies in bed while she rested. I wasn't sure if it was from all of the excitement yesterday morning or if she was coming down with something, but she seemed not to feel well today, which had me concerned. She was away from us long enough for someone to have given her something, even though she insisted no one had.

"Yes, I think he is." Mike pulled the chair out and sat down beside me. "I think several people are involved, and honestly, I'm not sure who we can trust right now. The biggest connection to all of this is Justin."

"Justin?" I asked, my voice catching in my throat.

"He was the only one who pushed her to testify. That wasn't part of the job, Quinn. He was responsible for securing her until she went into witness protection and U.S. Marshals took over. If he hadn't kept pushing her, she might not have testified, and the case would have gone in a different direction."

"So you think someone is trying to take Rosie because her dad put a child sex trafficker behind bars?" I knew that was exactly what he was saying, but it felt better to hear the words out loud instead of rattling around in my brain.

"They're leaving clues directly related to him and the car accident. It's not them being sloppy. It's them sending a message."

I pulled in a shaky breath and held the picture in front of me. Elias Salvador was handsome—not as handsome as Roman—but handsome enough to get what he wanted from women without having to work for it. His dark eyes hid the evil that resided inside and was offset by a smile that could melt a nun's panties. It was unnerving to see a smile offered so freely in a mugshot photo as if he didn't have a care in the world. It wasn't the look that I was used to seeing of people who realized that life as they knew it was over because the rest of it would be spent behind bars.

I hated that he had been let out early and even more that he hadn't been given a long sentence to begin with. But it seemed that his father had been convicted of the majority of the crimes, and he was simply just another measly pawn in the game.

"So, what do we do now?" I asked, lowering the picture to the table, and sliding it back to Mike.

"We stay vigilant. Alert. We don't take our eyes off of Rosie, and we work as a team to protect her."

"Do you think they're coming for her soon?"

He shrugged and folded his arms over his chest.

"There's no way to know. But I don't think they're just going to back off and forget about her."

My stomach soured, and I could taste the bitterness of the bile as it rose up.

"I hate not knowing."

"I know. Me too." He gently squeezed my shoulder. "But we're going to keep her safe. Not to worry."

"Okay," I whispered.

Twenty-Three

Roman
5 Days Ago

"Is that really necessary?" I asked, standing in the living room with my arms folded.

Mike shifted the coffee table in front of the door and stepped back to look at his work.

"If anyone tries to get in, I want to make sure that we hear them."

"It's late. Can we just wrap this up so I can get Rosie to bed?" Quinn asked with her hands on her hips. "It's been a long day, and she has school tomorrow."

"Yeah, I'll be there in a minute. Go ahead and get her situated, you won't even hear me come in."

"Why are you coming to the bedroom?" Her brows pulled together tightly.

"I'm sleeping on the floor."

I rolled my head back on my neck and waited for the fight I knew was coming.

"Look," she said sternly, holding her hand up in front of her. "I know you want to be here to watch over Rosie and keep her safe, but I don't think that entails you sleeping on the floor. I'll be in there with her, and if anyone gets into the apartment, you guys will hear them before we do."

"Unless they come in through the window," he countered.

"What in the world makes you think someone is going to climb four flights of rickety stairs on the fire escape to get in through the window?"

"It happens all the time." He spread his feet, widening his stance as they continued their stare-off.

"When?" I asked, pulling my head back in surprise.

He tilted his head and looked at me. "Max said that Hannah's friend—"

"Was *thrown* from a window," I corrected, feeling satisfied when I saw the embarrassment flash across his face.

"Oh, yeah. That's right. There was a lot going on, and I didn't hear the full story."

I didn't bother to go into the details of how she was murdered by some psychopath that also kidnapped Max's sister before taking Hannah. Quinn had enough on her plate to worry about without the gruesome details of someone else's tragedy.

"You don't need to sleep on the floor," Quinn insisted.

"Why not? It's not like there's room out here."

"You can sleep in that chair," she said, nodding to the one beside the couch where I would be sleeping.

"I'm six-two, Quinn. How the hell do you think I'm going to fit in that thing to sleep?"

"Maybe you can curl up on the couch with Roman?"

I watched the sparkle that danced in her eyes when she cautiously glanced at me.

"Yeah—like hell he is."

"Why not?" Mike asked with a decent amount of hurt in his tone.

"Because I don't cuddle men, and even if I considered it to keep you from having to sleep in the chair, your snoring is enough to make me reconsider."

Quinn covered her mouth and snorted as a laugh escaped.

Mike's head whipped toward her before he pointed a finger between us.

"That's the real reason you don't want me in there—isn't it?"

Quinn's head fell back, showing off her long neck as her hair tickled her back and the beautiful sound of laughter floated through the air.

"It's sooo loud!"

"You know what—screw both of you," Mike said playfully, pretending to be angry without letting his laughter slip through.

After a few minutes, the laughter subsided and Quinn yawned. It was late, and I didn't want to spend the entire night trying to figure out sleeping arrangements with all of my new roommates. As long as we kept Rosie safe, that was all that mattered.

"You can take the couch tonight," I offered. "I'll sleep in the chair."

"That chair will hurt your back," Quinn protested.

"I'll be fine. Trust me, I've slept on worse."

"You're welcome to sleep in the room with us," she offered quietly, almost afraid to let Mike hear her.

He clutched a hand to his heart and acted wounded.

"You'll let him sleep in the room with you, but not your own brother? I'm appalled!"

"He doesn't snore like a freight train," she laughed. "We all need sleep, and that's the best way for us to get it."

"Fine," Mike grumbled and ran his hands through his hair. "But don't you try anything funny with her…."

He grabbed his duffle bag from the floor and headed to the bathroom, leaving Quinn and me in awkward silence.

Once he was gone and we heard the door close, we both relaxed.

"You don't have to sleep on the floor," she said softly. "I'm sure there's plenty of room for all three of us in the bed."

"Na, that's okay. I'll sleep better if I'm by the door. If anyone comes in through the window they'll have to break it first, and we'll hear it."

She nodded her head and started blinking rapidly to keep her tears away.

I stepped forward and pulled her into me, holding her tightly.

"It's going to be okay," I assured her. "Nothing is going to happen to her with all of us here tonight. It's best to get as much rest as possible so you're ready to go tomorrow. She can't afford for you to be exhausted."

"I know," she said, her words muffled against my chest. "I'm so scared."

I didn't say anything because anything that I would have said would have been a lie. I could've told her that there was nothing to be scared of or that we could handle anything that was thrown at us, but that wasn't something that I could guarantee. While I hoped we would be prepared for whatever happened, uncertainty gnawed at me, making me question everything I thought I knew.

Twenty-Four

Quinn

4 Days Ago

I missed the days of getting up and starting my day in peace and quiet while Rosie slept and no one was out trying to kidnap her. Instead, I was at Roman's apartment, waiting for my turn to take a shower while Mike finished his and Roman worked on making breakfast with the few groceries he had left.

It had only been a few days since he had gone grocery shopping, but I don't think he was prepared for how much three people would eat compared to how much food he usually went through. I felt bad that he was spending so much money on things for Rosie and me, but I hated even more that I didn't have any other options right now. My apartment had already been cleared to go back to, and a new door was installed to replace the one that had been kicked down, but it wasn't safe to take Rosie back, so we were staying with Roman for the unforeseeable future.

Once Mike was done in the shower, I jumped in and didn't bother to wash my hair since the water was already cold, and we were running out of time. Luckily I had taken the time at my mom's house yesterday to wash my hair and give Rosie a bath, which saved us a lot of time today. I pulled my hair up into a sleek ponytail and skipped any makeup. One quick check in the mirror confirmed that I had matching shoes, and that was the most I could ask for today.

"But I really want one," Rosie whined from the living room as I came down the hall.

"I don't think your mom does," Mike replied, sitting across from her as they ate their bowls of cereal. Roman was leaning against the counter, holding a cup of coffee with his ankles crossed and a smirk on his face.

"I could keep it at your place," Rosie offered, wiggling her eyebrows excitedly, earning a frown from Mike as he took another bite.

"What are they talking about?" I asked Roman quietly, reaching for a cup and filling it with what was left in the pot.

"She's trying to convince him to get a dog."

I smiled and took a sip, holding the cup with both hands to keep from dropping it.

"Tired?" he questioned, tilting his head, and studying me.

"A little," I lied. The truth was that I was exhausted and couldn't remember the last time I had even an ounce of energy. The days felt like they were starting to blend together, and I was quickly losing track of how much time had passed by.

"Was I snoring?" he asked, wincing as he tucked his head down and took another sip.

"Not as bad as that one," I joked, lifting my mug at Mike, who had stood up and was heading our way.

"You weren't even in the same room," he said, nudging me with his elbow.

"I still heard you," I objected.

"Me too," Roman added.

Mike opened his mouth to speak but snapped it shut when Rosie got up and carried her empty cereal bowl into the kitchen and set it on the counter.

"You were so loud, I thought there was a bear in here," she

said dramatically, widening her eyes.

"Just when I thought you were my favorite niece," he teased.

"I'm your *only* niece," she giggled as he picked her up and tickled her sides.

I took a long drink of coffee then looked up at the clock on the wall.

"Go get your backpack and put your shoes on," I called to Rosie. "We're going to be late again."

My boss had been on my ass last week about my recent tardiness, and I swore that this week would be better. It was barely Monday morning, and I was already failing on my word.

I tilted my head back and tossed the rest of my coffee back before realizing that I had underestimated how much was left. The warm liquid dripped down my chin and onto my white silk shirt.

"Son of a bitch," I cursed, setting my cup down and pulling the fabric away from my body. "I don't have time for this."

"Go get changed. I can take Rosie to school," Roman offered.

"It's okay, you don't have to do that."

I continued to blot at my shirt with a napkin, only making it worse.

Roman reached out and grabbed my hand to stop me.

"Quinn—go get changed. We'll make sure she gets to school."

I hung my head in defeat and waited for a few seconds to regain my composure.

"Thank you. I appreciate it."

I headed to the bedroom to change while Mike helped Rosie get her shoes on in the living room. A few minutes later, she hugged me and told me she loved me before heading to school with two of the best bodyguards any little girl could ever ask for.

By six, I had worked through lunch and sat through hours of needless meetings that put me even further behind on my work. My mom had picked Rosie up from school an hour after the guys had dropped her off when she spiked a fever and started throwing up. The nurse made sure to call me before my mom got there to update me on how she was feeling.

After my mom got her home and comfortable, she sent me hourly updates with pictures of Rosie sleeping on the couch. The curtains were closed, which helped keep the room dark for her but increased my anxiety about not knowing whether the van was back again. Thankfully, my sister Sonia had the day off and was hanging out there to help keep an eye on everything. On top of that, Max had gone by to check on things as well. It was nice to feel the level of support we had right now, but it was still unsettling that the threat wasn't over.

I checked in with Roman to see if he was already home or if he wanted to go to my mom's to pick up Rosie with me. He was stuck at work for a little while longer, so I packed up and headed over there to wait for him so we could go home together and grab Rosie on the way.

It was relatively empty when I got to his work. I nodded to the guy at the front desk before making my way back to his office. He was on the phone when I walked in, so I set my stuff down and headed to the workout area to give him some privacy.

There were a handful of guys lifting weights in one room, but no one in the room with the punching bag. I looked around until I found a set of gloves and put them on. It had been a long time since I had hit anything and I felt the sting in my muscles with the first few punches I threw.

The moment my fists made contact with the bag, I felt this immediate sense of satisfaction that increased with each punch. I tucked my head and squared my shoulders, twisting my torso as I rotated hitting with each hand. I pictured Elias

Salvador and his disgusting father, Juan, and kept punching. Then I imagined Julia's face and her smug smile when she *brought* my daughter back and punched even harder. The more I thought about everything that was happening, the faster I hit until I was struggling to catch my breath and felt a set of muscular arms wrap around me from behind and cover my gloved hands so I couldn't hit anymore.

He didn't say anything, just kept his arms wrapped around me in a layer of comfort. My heart was racing, and my body was on fire as I came down from the adrenaline rush I had given myself. I knew that it hadn't solved anything, but for a few minutes, I felt better letting some of my built-up aggression out.

My body trembled as a range of emotions coursed through me. I tried to keep my composure but couldn't stop the tears before they rushed down my face. I didn't want Roman to see me like this and pushed against his arms to get away, but he only held on tighter. The tears burned my cheeks as they stained my face and ran down onto my shirt.

I leaned my head back against his chest and cried until there was nothing left inside. With a shaky breath, I tried to speak, but the words wouldn't come out. I had no idea what to say to him. His arms loosened around me and slid down to my waist, allowing me the freedom to slip the gloves off.

"I'm sorry," I whispered, turning to leave when his arm reached out and held my waist.

"You have nothing to apologize for."

I stopped where I was, letting his hand rest firmly against my stomach, and looked up at him.

His brown eyes clouded with emotion and I couldn't tell what he was thinking. Before I could overthink anything, he dug his fingers into my side and pulled me back to him. I stumbled briefly before he had both hands planted on my hips and his chest braced against mine.

I looked up at him, knowing that he felt the electricity sizzling between us. He muttered a curse word before leaning in and planting his lips on mine.

"You're going to be the death of me," he groaned before sliding his hands down to grab my ass.

I kissed him back and didn't allow myself to worry about anything else for the few minutes we had before we left to pick up Rosie.

Twenty-Five

Roman

4 Days Ago

My lips pressed hungrily against Quinn's, capturing the whispered moans that escaped her mouth. I wasn't lying when I said that she would be the death of me. Either we would finally act on this spark between us and Mike would kill me, or I would die from blue balls. One way or another, I was a goner.

Her fingers ran through my hair, lightly tugging on the short locks as she deepened the kiss.

"Quinn," I moaned, squeezing her ass as I lifted her to my waist and pressed her back to the wall.

"Mmmm," she answered, grinding her hips against my groin, and creating a friction that was sure to start a fire. "I want you, Roman. Now. Please."

I pulled away, breaking the kiss, and rested my forehead against hers while her fingers anxiously dug into the bottom of my shirt, trying to free me of it.

"Are you sure?"

"Yes," she panted.

"I don't want you to do this because you're upset."

"I'm not. I want you to fuck me, Roman. I have since I was sixteen and you spent the summer at our house playing basketball without your shirt on. You've been driving me wild ever since, and now you're like an itch that I desperately want to scratch."

I leaned in and kissed her, feeling my cheeks splitting into a smile.

"You've wanted me that long?" I asked, relieved that she had felt the same way I had.

"And longer since you're hellbent on making me wait more."

Her hands moved down, working my belt and zipper while I held her against the wall.

"Such a feisty little thing, aren't you?"

I heard the thud as my jeans hit the floor and smiled when she hooked her thumbs into the top of my briefs and tugged them down. My erection sprung free, touching my stomach as her hand glided over it.

I adjusted her on my hips and pushed her skirt up her thighs, revealing a black lace thong underneath. I bunched the fabric as high as I could so it was out of the way and then ran my hand across her pussy, feeling the warmth coming from it.

She closed her eyes and moaned as I traced circles with my fingers before pushing the thin material to the side and parting her. A gasp floated past her lips as she arched her back, giving me complete access as my finger slid easily between her folds.

"Fuck, Quinn," I breathed.

"Told you I was ready."

I wanted to keep fingering her, to feel her body spasm as she lost control, but my rock-hard cock was begging for attention, and the way Quinn's nails dug into my back said she felt the same way.

I was about to lower her to the floor so I could grab my wallet when I suddenly realized that I didn't have a condom.

"Fuck!" I cursed, closing my eyes and tossing my head back in frustration.

"What?"

"I don't have a condom."

I shook my head and then opened my eyes to find Quinn studying me while she nervously chewed her bottom lip.

"I'm on the pill," she said cautiously. "And I haven't been with anyone since Justin. I'm clean."

My heart fluttered at the thought of being with her without using protection, wondering what it would feel like.

"I've never been with a woman without using one," I replied gently. "I'm clean too. I get checked every year and haven't been with anyone in at least six months."

She nodded and took a slow, deep breath.

"Then what are we waiting for?" she asked, the sparkle back in her eyes.

A carnal growl escaped my lips before I pressed them to Quinn's and lined myself up at her opening. Her legs parted further, allowing me to slide inside easily. She was so wet that she welcomed my dick without any hesitation.

I pushed deeper inside, feeling her pussy clench around me as a hiss fell through her parted lips. She arched her back and swiveled her hips in circles, grinding against me as I thrust. My fingers dug into her ass cheeks, holding onto her as we rocked into each other.

Thankfully I had already checked that everyone had left before I walked the last few guys out and locked up, so I didn't have to worry about anyone walking in on us.

"I want to fuck you from behind," I moaned in her ear as I kept thrusting. She scratched her nails down my back and panted heavily.

"Okay," she breathed.

Slowly, I pulled out and helped her to her feet before walking her over to one of the weight benches in the other room. I stepped out of my shoes and tossed my clothes to the side before grabbing a clean towel from the closet and laying it on the seat before she bent over and popped her ass in the air. Her pussy glistened in the light and that was all that I needed to dive back in.

Her chest rested on the seat while her hands held onto the sides to keep from falling off. I spread my feet slightly and lined up at her entrance, making sure to ease into her slowly so I didn't knock her over. Once I was inside, she started bucking against me, meeting me thrust for thrust as I reached down and rubbed her clit with my finger.

Watching her tight ass as it bounced against my cock was enough to make me want to come right then and there. Add in the incredible sensation of feeling her wet pussy clenching around me without a condom, and I was going to embarrass myself with how long I lasted.

"Fuck me harder," she whispered, looking at me over her shoulder.

Our eyes locked and I grabbed onto her hips, plowing into her as hard as I could while she held on for dear life with one hand and reached down to touch herself with the other.

I held my breath and counted to twenty to keep from coming right away, but when she clenched around me as her orgasm ripped through her, I had no choice but to let go and succumb to mine.

My hips jerked rapidly as my cock twitched inside her, my cum shooting through her before I pulled out, and she collapsed on the bench. I ran a hand across her naked ass, the site a beautiful one with her skirt still bunched around her waist and her heels still on.

I grabbed my briefs and jeans, slipping them on before heading to the bathroom. I grabbed a washcloth on the way and ran it under warm water. Quinn was sitting on the bench when I got back, checking her phone.

"Everything okay?" I asked as I sat down next to her.

"Yeah, I was just checking on Rosie. My mom said she's still sleeping so we don't have to rush over there."

I nodded and held up the washcloth. She arched an eyebrow and tilted her head slightly.

"Lay down," I instructed.

"Why?"

"So I can take care of my mess."

"You don't have to do that. I can go to the bathroom and take care of it."

"Quinn."

She sighed heavily and laid down, her body surprisingly rigid, given the orgasm she had a few minutes ago.

I turned my body and gently pushed her legs open, letting my hand skim the inside of her thigh. I chuckled when I realized that we had been so caught up in the moment that I never bothered to take her panties off; we just pushed them to the side. She had since then fixed them, but I could see the evidence of what we had done on them.

I hooked my finger in them and gently slid them off of her.

"What are you doing?" she asked, popping her head up to look at me.

"Trust me, I don't think you want to wear those anymore."

She giggled and laid back down while I gently cleaned her up. Once I was done, I leaned forward and gently kissed her clit, loving the way she smelled right now. I knew that we had already used more time than we had so I couldn't go down on her like I wanted to.

She squirmed beneath me and held my head between her legs while I took a few seconds to lick her lips and taste her. I worked my way back up to her clit and gave it a quick flick with my tongue, causing her to gasp.

"Soooo sensitive," she murmured.

I laughed and sat up, pulling her hands to help her up.

"We don't have time right now but trust me when I say that I'm going to eat that sweet pussy of yours as soon as I can."

"Is that a threat or a promise?"

"Both."

Twenty-Six

Quinn

3 Days Ago

My body was mind-numbingly sore when I woke up, but I wasn't about to complain when I had one of the most life-altering orgasms of my life last night. I knew that being with Roman would be amazing, but I had no idea it would be that incredible.

We got back to his apartment shortly after nine, and I knew that Mike was suspicious when he was there waiting for us at my mom's house. We both lied so quickly that neither of us could get our stories straight as to why we were late. My mom was more concerned about why I had been crying, which helped pull Mike's attention away from the fact that Roman had a small hickey on his neck where I had let my desire get the best of me before he took me from behind on the weight bench.

Rosie stayed asleep the entire time as Mike carried her to Roman's apartment, refusing to let him help. We got her settled in, and I spent most of the night watching over her to make sure her fever didn't spike again. I cuddled her close to me and let her soft snores help me drift off to sleep around two in the morning.

Roman had offered to sleep on the floor again, but Mike quickly squashed that idea—as if there was any real threat to having him in the same room with me if Rosie was there. I might have been head over heels obsessed with Roman right now, but I wasn't about to throw my panties at him with my daughter in the same room. Instead, they both slept in the living room and compromised on who would sleep on the floor in the sleeping bag that Mike had brought from my mom's house.

I stretched and rolled out of bed, making sure I didn't disturb Rosie. She had gotten up around five this morning, throwing up again, so I gave her some more Tylenol for her fever and got her back to bed. I snuck down the hall, closing the door behind me, and stopped when I realized that I couldn't go to the living room to call the school without waking Mike and Roman up.

Instead, I snuck into the bathroom and quietly closed the door behind me. I called the school and left a voicemail to let them know that Rosie was sick and wouldn't be in today. Then I sent my mom a quick text message with an update on how she was feeling. I didn't want to miss work, but I was so exhausted and worn down that I decided it was better to be home to take care of Rosie.

Once I had taken care of calling in, I opened the bathroom door and jumped back in surprise when I found Roman on the other side. I held my phone to my chest and tried to get my heart to stop racing.

"Sorry," he said quietly. "Someday, I'm going to get a bigger place with two bathrooms." He grinned, showing me his beautiful dimples.

"I promise we won't be here that much longer."

It was an odd feeling to promise something that I didn't know if it was true.

"You can stay as long as you'd like."

His voice was smooth like honey, and the way he was looking at me had the heat between my thighs starting again.

"Thank you," I said quietly, looking down as my face blushed. "I'm sure you'd like to have your space back and have some privacy again."

"I don't need privacy."

"Oh?" My voice hitched in my throat, the words getting lodged there.

He shook his head and licked his lips.

Before I could say anything more, I heard footsteps right as a hand reached out and clamped down on Roman's shoulder.

"What's going on?" he asked, looking between us.

"I was asking Quinn how Rosie was feeling," Roman answered without missing a beat, his eyes still locked on mine.

I looked away, not trusting myself to look at him while my brother was standing there, looking ready to murder him.

"She's still sick and had a restless night. Her fever wasn't as high this morning, but she's still running one. I called the school and told them that she wouldn't be there today."

"I can miss work to stay with her," Mike offered.

"That's okay, I already called in. I have some PTO that I can use."

"I can stay with her too," Roman said simultaneously, causing Mike to look between us.

"What's going on between you two?" he asked, pointing a finger.

"Nothing," I lied.

I didn't want to lie, but the last thing I needed right now was to deal with my brother and risk a falling out between him and Roman.

Roman rubbed a hand across the back of his neck and looked away.

"Bullshit."

I swallowed hard. This was not how I wanted him to find out.

"Are you two fucki—"

"Mommy, I don't feel well," Rosie said, standing in the doorway rubbing her eyes.

I pushed past Mike and went to her, pulling her into me as I laid my hand on her forehead to check her temperature.

"You're burning up again," I confirmed, tilting my head to see her face. "Let's get you a cold washcloth and some water."

"Did the Tylenol not help?" Roman asked as he and Mike followed us into the living room. Mike hurried in to move the blankets off of the couch so she could sit down.

"It doesn't seem like it. I gave it to her an hour ago."

"What do you need?" Mike asked as we all headed into the kitchen while Rosie sat on the couch and curled into a ball.

I closed my eyes and tried to force myself to focus. I was exhausted. But I knew that we would need the basics—at minimum—and I didn't have a way to go out to get them. On top of that, we were running low on clean clothes after she got sick again last night. My mom had a pile of clothes at her house that she was planning to wash for me today, but there wasn't a way for me to run over there to get them.

"Um," I said, pinching the bridge of my nose while I thought about it. "I need stuff for Rosie—more children's Tylenol, Gatorade, crackers, and maybe some soup. Unfortunately, I can't think straight, so I have no idea what I'm missing."

I looked between them, feeling loved and supported by how they were watching me.

"I'll go to the store and grab some groceries plus the stuff you listed. Is there anything you want for yourself?" Roman asked.

"I'm fine but thank you."

He furrowed his brow but didn't fight me on it.

"I have some clothes at Mom's that she was washing for me," I said, turning to Mike. "I don't know if you can grab them on your way home tonight or if it's out of the—"

"I'll get them, don't worry about it."

"Thank you. Both of you are tremendously helpful."

Rosie started coughing, which pulled my attention away from the guys while I went to check on her. I grabbed a cold bottle of water from the fridge and offered it to her, hoping to get some fluid into her.

She took slow sips of water and then handed the bottle back to me.

"How are you feeling?" I asked, pressing the back of my hand to her forehead. She still felt warm but not as hot as she was a few minutes ago.

"I'm sleepy."

"Why don't you lay down and get some rest? I'll be right here if you need anything."

"Okay, mommy."

She scooted down on the couch and curled into the pillow, her head barely touching it before her eyes fluttered closed. I snuck to the bathroom and grabbed the thermometer, then carefully scanned her head to get her temperature. 99.2.

I sighed a breath of relief that it had come down some and was no longer sitting in the 100-101 range that it had been most of the night. I prayed that the Tylenol was working and that the rest would give her body what she needed to fight whatever this was.

When I went back to the kitchen, the guys were talking quietly while Roman wrote down whatever Mike was telling him.

"Be sure to get the ones in the red bag," Mike said, pointing to something on the paper.

"What are you doing?" I asked, standing on my tiptoes to look over Roman's shoulder.

"Just making a list," he replied, turning away from me to keep me from seeing it.

"Anything else?" he asked Mike, completely ignoring me.

"I think that's it. I'll grab the other stuff on my way back."

"Your way back?" My eyebrows raised off my forehead.

"Yeah, I'm working a half-day today."

"Why?"

"So I can help take care of you and Rosie."

"I don't need help, Mike. I'm fine. Really."

"You're exhausted, Quinn," Roman said gently.

"So?"

"How are you supposed to take care of a sick child when you're so worn down? It would be good for you to rest too." Mike added.

"I do it all the time and have since she was a baby." I folded my arms and narrowed my eyes defensively at him.

"That's not what I meant," he blew out, running a hand through his hair. "I know that you've been doing it since she was born—and you do an amazing job. I just meant that this time it's different because… well, you know…."

"Because someone is trying to kidnap my daughter, and I might be too tired to fight them off if they try?"

"Exactly." Roman's voice was hard but not harsh. "We can't take any chances right now, Quinn. So please, just let us help you."

"Fine," I sighed. It wasn't the worst idea in the world; I just hated that Mike would have to miss work because of me. "I guess missing half a day at work isn't too terrible." I smiled at my brother and then added, "thank you."

"Good, well, I'm glad that we got that settled. Roman is going to run to the store to grab some groceries, and then when he gets back, I'll head to the office. After that, I'll run by Mom's and grab the laundry, but she said to let her know if you need it before then, and she can run by here and drop it off."

"Wait," I said, holding my hand up. "What do you mean when Roman gets back?"

"I called in today too."

"You don't have to do that."

"Quinn…." My name was a warning on his lips, and I knew better than to fight it.

"Fine. But make sure to pick up some more coffee while you're out. I have a feeling I'm going to need it."

I yawned and headed over to the other end of the couch and curled up next to Rosie, lifting her legs to rest on my lap so she had enough room. It was warm in the apartment, but suddenly, I felt chilly, so I grabbed a blanket from the floor beside me and covered up.

Roman gave a quick nod before slipping out the door and closing it behind him. Mike poured himself another cup of coffee before getting a phone call that he rushed to the bathroom to answer. Alone in the peace and quiet, I closed my eyes and laid my head against the cushion.

I had no idea how long I had been asleep before Mike gently shook my shoulder and woke me up.

"Hey, sorry to wake you, but I need to head to the office,

and Roman isn't back yet. Will you be okay for a little bit on your own?"

"Yeah, of course. We'll be fine." I looked over at Rosie, sound asleep and gently snoring again.

"Okay. If you need anything, call me on my cell and keep calling until I answer. I mean it, Quinn—anything at all."

"I'll be okay, and I'm sure Roman won't be gone much longer."

He glanced down at his watch and then checked his phone.

"I thought he would be back already, but apparently, it's taking longer than we thought. I sent him a text message, but he hasn't gotten back to me."

"I'll have him reach out as soon as he gets back."

"Okay." He looked at Rosie and me again, seeming to struggle with his decision to leave.

"Go," I coaxed, shooing him away.

Finally, he grabbed his keys from the table and left.

I closed my eyes and willed myself to stay awake, but they felt so heavy. I couldn't remember the last time that I had slept so well, and my body desperately craved it.

I felt numb, like I was floating through the clouds, weightless and without any worries. A long, flowy white dress covered my body, twirling freely as I spun in circles, dancing to a song that only I could hear. Everything felt right as I kept spinning, laughing the faster I went.

Then suddenly, I hit something hard, and it jolted me out of my bliss. I looked around, trying to find what I had crashed into. There was bright light blinding me as I lifted my hand to try to shield it. Suddenly it went away and standing before me was Justin.

There was a cut on his forehead with blood dripping from it. Instinctively I reached up to wipe it away but pulled my hand back when it went right through him. He wasn't really there. I reached for him again, disappointed when the same thing happened. Slowly he started to fade away, being pulled into a darkness that I couldn't see.

"Justin!" I called out, picking up the bottom of my dress to run after him.

My feet hurt from stepping on the shards of broken glass. There were thick trees around me, casting the shadows that hid him.

"Justin!" I cried out again. My heart raced as I tried to run faster, desperate to find him. He needed help. He needed me.

I kept running, tripping over pieces of debris but not realizing what it was until I got to a single tree in the middle of nowhere. I looked around and gasped, covering my mouth as the tears dripped down my face.

A horn blared off in the distance, but I couldn't see it. Instead, my eyes were fixated on the image of Justin hanging from one of the tree branches with a seat belt wrapped around his neck.

I jolted upright, nearly launching myself off the couch as I tried to shake the image out of my head. My palms were sweaty, and my heart was racing so loud that I could hear the blood pulsing through my ears.

I leaned forward, trying to catch my breath when I heard the doorknob turn. Relieved that Roman was home, I got up and started walking to the door, then stopped when I realized that it wasn't Roman.

Twenty-Seven

Quinn

3 Days Ago

I watched the doorknob rattle a few times before I jumped up and pushed the coffee table across the room, forcing it in front of the door. It was heavy enough to stop whoever it was from getting in for a few seconds while I grabbed my gun. I glanced at Rosie, making sure she was still asleep before running down the hall to the bedroom. I stood on my tiptoes and retrieved my gun from the top shelf of Roman's closet where I had been keeping it.

My footsteps were light but quick as I went back to the living room, gun aimed at the door and hands steady in front of me. I waited for a few seconds before I inched closer, wishing that I had brought my bulletproof vest home. There wasn't time to worry about that right now. Someone was still on the other side of the door, trying to pick the lock.

Rosie snored loudly and rolled over, pulling my attention to her for a brief second. When I looked back at the door, it was being forced open as someone rammed their body into it.

A few seconds later, the wood splintered around the body that burst through the door. Whoever it was had a ski mask covering their face and was dressed in all black, making it impossible to see anything.

Instinctively, I moved in front of Rosie, shielding her from them as I kept my gun aimed at their head.

"Don't come one step closer," I commanded.

They tilted their head and looked past me. I moved again, keeping her hidden.

"Get out now," I warned as my fingers tightened around the trigger.

I studied them and tried to lock away as many details in my mind as I could. The way they stood, their height and weight—things that would be easy to identify later.

They moved quickly, darting for the couch. I kept my eyes focused on them as I pulled the trigger.

After three shots, I lowered my gun and watched them sink to the floor, clutching their shoulder. I reached for my phone to call for help when I heard Rosie crying behind me.

I turned around and found her curled into a ball on the couch, crying and shaking as she looked at the body on the ground in front of me.

Quickly, I tucked my gun into my pants and rushed over to her.

"Shhh, honey, it's okay." I grabbed her and clutched her to my chest, holding her tightly as she cried.

I hated that she had to witness this, but I hated even more that I had allowed myself to be distracted for a split second and that it allowed whoever it was to get away. There was a trail of blood that led to the open doorway where Roman now stood, jaw hanging open and grocery bags stacked on both arms.

"What happened?"

Twenty-Eight

Roman

3 Days Ago

"What the hell happened?" I asked again, tossing the bags to the counter before rushing over to Quinn and Rosie.

Rosie was sobbing uncontrollably as Quinn held her. I looked down at the blood smeared on the floor and then up at Quinn, needing answers from her.

"Someone got in," she said quietly.

I raised my brows, asking the question I didn't want Rosie to hear.

She shook her head.

"Three shots to the chest and shoulder."

My head was spinning while I put everything together. Had I been here, none of this would have happened. First of all— no one would have gotten through the door. Second—they wouldn't have left with a gunshot wound.

Quinn held and rocked Rosie, slowly calming her down. I went to the kitchen and put the groceries away, knowing that we wouldn't need them here after all. There was no way that I could keep them safe with splintered wood for a door.

I pulled out my phone and called Mike, waiting for him to pick up and answer. By the third time, I was starting to get annoyed when he answered and huffed out, "now isn't a good time, man."

"Yeah, same here."

"What do you mean? What happened? Is Rosie okay?" His tone immediately changed, and whatever had him stressed out a few seconds ago was now replaced with another source of worry.

"Someone just broke into my apartment."

"Fuck. Are they okay?"

"Yeah, Quinn handled it."

I didn't want to get into the details about it now, and honestly, I didn't trust Mike's phone not to be bugged, given everything else that was happening. "What's going on with you?"

"Saul Gomez was just rushed to the hospital. He was shot."

"Where?" My throat was tight, and my jaw clenched. This had to be it—we had our guy. I knew that bastard was after Rosie from the moment I laid eyes on him holding her shoulder at Sandra's house when he was supposedly helping her find the bathroom.

"Leg and abdomen. He was grabbing lunch; it was a drive-by shooting."

"Was anyone else with him?"

"Not that I know of. We're still waiting for more information. He's in surgery now."

I chewed the inside of my cheek, frustrated that it was starting to sound more like a coincidence than anything.

"Any chance he was also shot in the shoulder or chest?" I asked.

"Not that I heard, why?"

"Because someone left my apartment with three bullets that your sister put into them."

Twenty-Nine

Quinn

2 Days Ago

"If I never have to pack again, I'll be forever grateful," I muttered as I tossed a duffle bag of clothes onto the guest bed at Mike's apartment.

"It's only for a little while," he said gently, leaning against the doorframe with his arms folded over his chest. We both knew it was true, given that neither my apartment nor Roman's was safe anymore; he was the last resort on such short notice. But we also knew it wasn't safe for long; whoever it was would find us here too. That was why we didn't go to my mom's house. I wanted to keep her safe, which meant that we needed to avoid her and Sonia at this point. It was too dangerous to get them involved by staying with them.

"That was supposed to be true about Roman too. I was only supposed to stay there for a few nights, and almost two weeks later, we were still there. I just want to go back to my own apartment and go back to normal."

"I know," he sighed. "But unfortunately, that's not an option right now. We have to keep you and Rosie safe."

"Safe?" I snorted, tossing my phone on the bed. "Do you really think that we're going to be safe anywhere? Whoever it is keeps finding us wherever we go, so I don't see why we can't just go back to my apartment and be comfortable. I'm so tired," I said, rubbing my eyes. "I don't want to keep running and looking over my shoulder."

"The only way around that is to relocate you guys."

"Like through witness protection?"

He shrugged.

"The department that my husband worked for and died on the job? The same department that you work for that seems to have a mole?"

"Technically, it wouldn't need to go through us at all. US Marshals handle witness protection. I have a friend who I trust that I could ask for a favor."

"Mike, you and I both know that neither of us can ask for any favors right now without someone getting wind of it. We don't know who we can or can't trust. There's too much at stake right now to risk it."

"So then you're stuck with me for a while?"

"It looks that way," I said with a soft laugh.

We stayed quiet for a few minutes before he pushed off the wall and ran a hand through his hair.

"I'm going to do everything I can to keep her safe, Quinn. I promise you that. No one is leaving you alone in the apartment again."

"So we're all just quitting our jobs and living here together?" My brows rose high on my head.

"It's not forever. Whoever it is, is getting restless. They're making more attempts. We just need to catch them and end this."

I tried to smile, but it disappeared before it hit my lips. Mike's phone rang, pulling him into the hallway to answer it. We were still waiting for an update on Saul—who had been seen at a food truck a few blocks away from the office when he was shot, which ruled him out from being the same person who broke into Roman's apartment.

"Yeah, okay. I'm on my way." Mike hung up and shoved his phone back into his pocket as he came back into the guest room. "I need to go meet Max to discuss a few things. Roman is in the kitchen with Rosie. I'll grab some groceries on my way back, but Mom is headed over with a few casseroles in the meantime."

"Okay," I nodded. "Thank you."

He smiled, then turned and left. I fell back on the bed and laid there for a few minutes, pretending that my life wasn't currently one big dumpster fire.

An hour later, my mom had shown up with my sister Sonia and a week's worth of meals to go in the freezer. On top of that, she had a pan of chicken enchiladas, beans, and rice that were hot and ready to eat. We sat down at the small table in Mike's kitchen and ate dinner together as a family.

Once we were done, my mom took Rosie to give her a bath while I helped Roman clean up. Sonia was helping blow up the air mattress that they brought for Roman to sleep on. It was amazing how much help and support we had, though I hated the reason why we needed it.

"How are you holding up?" Roman asked, gently bumping my shoulder with his as I rinsed the plate and set it in the dishwasher.

"I've been better, and I've been worse," I said with a shrug. "So, I guess I'm somewhere in between?"

Yesterday had been a long day dealing with multiple agencies over the shooting. While we didn't have to worry about proof that someone had tried to break in and that I fired my gun in self-defense—it sucked that we didn't have anyone in custody nor a suspect to go after.

"Have they heard anything about Saul?" I asked, looking up at him as he handed me another plate.

"Mike said that he was out of surgery but then took a turn for the worse and was rushed back into another one. I haven't heard anything since then."

"It's so crazy," I muttered.

I added the last few dishes to the dishwasher and then started it. My body was sore and tired as I leaned against the counter behind me.

"I just wish all of this was over already. Or better yet—I wish it wasn't happening to begin with."

"Me too. But we'll keep both of you safe." He took a deep breath and then sighed heavily. "I know that probably doesn't mean much given what happened yesterday…." His head dropped as his hand shot through his short, dark hair.

"Hey," I said gently, pulling his hand down. "That wasn't your fault."

He let his hand drop, our fingers entwining in the process. I turned toward him, pressing my chest into his as his hand snaked around my waist and pulled me tighter.

"I should have been there. I hate that I wasn't."

"You didn't know."

"We knew there was a threat—that's all I needed to know. Instead, I was off looking for something and got distracted. I know better than to let myself lose focus."

"What were you looking for?" My curiosity getting the best of me.

He let go of me for a brief moment as he walked over and grabbed his backpack from the hook by the door. A few minutes later, he came back and handed me a bag of gummy worms.

The corners of my lips turned up as I held it, realizing that this was what he and Mike had been talking about yesterday when I overheard them. I didn't eat a lot of sweets, but gummy worms were my weakness, and the ones in the red bag were my favorite.

"They were out at the market that I went to, so I went to a few other places before I finally found them," he explained.

I held them to my chest and looked up at him, trying to blink away the tears.

"You didn't have to do that."

"I wanted to. I mean, it was originally Mike's idea to get them, but I was the one who had asked him what your favorite snack was."

I wrapped my arms around his neck, careful not to scratch him with the bag. My eyes fluttered closed as my lips brushed against his before they parted, and his tongue swiped against mine.

"You're so sweet," I whispered between kisses.

He pulled away and slowly trailed his lips down the side of my neck. "I wanted to do something nice for you." His teeth gently nipped my skin. "You've had so much going on and needed a treat."

"I had a nice treat the other night," I giggled playfully as I scratched my nails up his back under his shirt. "But this is great too."

"Are you saying that sex with me is comparable to gummy worms?" He pulled back and raised a dark brow at me.

"Well," I laughed. "Both are pretty satisfying."

"But has a candy ever made you come before?" he whispered by my ear, the coarse hair on his chin teasing my skin.

"Hmmm," I teased, playfully tapping my finger to my chin. "I'm not going to answer—"

"What the fuck is this?" Mike's voice boomed from the front door before it slammed shut behind him.

I immediately jumped back, putting enough space between us to douse the flame that was starting to build between my legs.

"It's not what it looks like," I lied quietly, lowering my head to avoid his heated gaze. I wasn't afraid of much, but that didn't mean that I wanted to see my brother's disappointment etched on his face. I could still hear Rosie laughing from the bathroom with my mom, so I knew she wasn't headed out here yet.

"It is what it looks like," Roman confirmed, digging his fingers into my hip and pulling me toward him protectively.

"Is it?" Mike questioned, standing in front of us with his feet spread shoulder-width apart and arms crossed. "Because it looks like you're fucking my sister."

"Mike!" I covered my mouth with my hand, not sure if I was more embarrassed that my older brother knew that I was doing his best friend or if it was hearing the words come out of his mouth.

"Like I said," Roman said with a shrug.

"I warned you," Mike bit out, taking a few steps toward us.

"Yeah. And?" Roman quipped, stepping in front of me and putting a hand behind him to keep me in place. "What are you going to do, Mike? Try to kick my ass because I fell for your sister and we acted on impulse like two *very* consensual adults?"

"Oh, I'm gonna do more than *try* to kick your ass."

"Let's see what you've got."

I watched as they stood chest to chest, both of them fuming so hot that I was surprised I didn't see smoke coming out of their ears.

"That's enough," I hissed, pushing in between them. "We have enough going on right now; we don't need to add this to the mix."

"I was just going to say the same thing," Mike replied while looking over at me and keeping his eyes on Roman. "Seems like a bad time to start a new *relationship*, given everything else that's going on. And I know that my *best friend* wouldn't be using my sister as a fuck buddy—so obviously, there's a relationship that you guys haven't told anyone about."

I could feel the heavy breath from Roman behind me and knew that he was trying to stay calm.

"You don't know shit—"

"I will handle this," I said, lifting my hand to stop him.

I waited for Mike to stop glaring at Roman and look at me before I spoke.

"Mike, I love that you're still my protective big brother after all of these years, but this isn't something that you need to be concerned with."

"But—"

"Nope. You do NOT get a say in any of this. I am a grown woman and know exactly what I'm getting myself into with Roman. You don't need to step in and protect me when you know damn well that he's a good guy. If he's good enough to be your best friend all of these years, then I don't see why you wouldn't think that he was good enough for me. Wouldn't you want someone like him for your sister? Someone that you know and trust?"

I tilted my head and studied him, pinning him with a look. "Or do I not deserve that?"

He pulled his head back and scowled.

"You know you deserve more than that, Quinn. You deserve more than anyone could ever give you."

"So then, are you saying that Roman isn't good enough for me?"

He looked from me to his best friend, his face softening some.

"I didn't say that."

I released a frustrated breath and forced my shoulders down.

"Well, that's what you're insinuating, and it's just as rude to him as it is to me. I know that you love both of us and care about our happiness, but you need to step back and realize that this is none of your business. Whatever happens between Roman and me is for us to handle—not you."

"I don't want to be caught in the middle if things go south between you guys."

"Then don't. No one is forcing you to be in that position. Before this, Roman and I saw each other at random holidays—it's not like we were constantly around each other. I'd like to believe that someday things will return to a somewhat normal state, and God forbid—if something did happen and we couldn't be around each other—we're adults who can act civil and move on with our lives. It's a shame you don't trust us enough to let us try this and see what happens. It could be something really wonderful." I stepped back and leaned into Roman's side as he wrapped an arm around me.

Mike looked between us, watching the way we held each other.

"So," he said with his jaw still clenched. "This is happening?"

We both nodded.

"Fine," he sighed. "But absolutely no sex under my roof."

He turned and walked out of the room, muttering something under his breath as he worked his tie free from his neck.

Thirty

Roman

1 Day Ago

I slept like shit last night, but that was nothing new. Ever since Quinn showed up, asking for my help a few weeks ago, I hadn't relaxed enough to truly rest. I had debated going back to my apartment to handle things but decided to stay at Mike's place after agreeing that it was better to keep Rosie safe by having more eyes on her.

Quinn and Rosie slept in the guest bedroom while Mike stayed awake in his, and I camped out on the couch in the living room. He had gotten a call around five this morning, confirming that Saul had more complications during surgery and didn't make it.

I was in the kitchen, brewing a pot of coffee when there was a knock on Mike's door. Before I could answer it, he came down the hallway, looking at me, confused. I shrugged, not having any clue who was there, and then went back to grabbing some mugs from the hooks above the sink.

"What do you want?" he asked, slowly opening the door but not enough to let in whoever was on the other side.

"I need to talk to you," a quiet female voice answered.

"Now isn't a good time. We can talk at the office."

"You don't understand, Mike—there isn't going to be a good time. This is urgent."

The door pushed open, and the woman from the party that Mike hated appeared. I pushed at the corners of my mind, trying to recall her name, but the lack of sleep had me struggling this morning.

"Anastasia," he groaned, shoving a hand through his hair in frustration.

"Look—I know that you don't like me and hate having to deal with me, but there's something that you need to know."

"What?"

I leaned against the counter, not making any effort to leave as she tossed her honey blonde hair over her shoulder, and her hazel eyes pleaded with him to listen.

"Frank Bestillos was murdered this morning. They found his body when a neighbor called the apartment manager about a noise complaint. The door was kicked open, and his body was left in the kitchen, bullet to the head."

"What the fuck?" Mike muttered, shaking his head in disbelief.

"That's not all," she said nervously. "Julia was taken to the hospital this morning. Someone attacked her on her way to work in an alley. An onlooker intervened and scared them off before they could do anything else."

I pushed off the counter and joined them.

"Are these all the same people who—"

"Were in the car when Justin died." Mike pulled his lips into a thin line.

"So someone's taking out his entire team?"

She nodded as tears filled her eyes.

"Do you think it's Elias Salvador?" I asked. "It seems pretty convenient that suddenly everyone that was working the case that sent him and his father to prison is now being targeted and murdered."

"I don't know what to do," she whispered. "I can't shake the feeling that something terrible is about to happen. I didn't want to bother you by coming here, but since Justin was your brother-in-law, I was worried they might come for you too."

Before he could say anything, I noticed the red dot that quickly moved from her forehead to her chest, then back up again.

"Get down now!" I shouted, diving toward her and pulling her to the floor as a bullet whipped past us. Mike crouched next to me before taking off toward the guest bedroom where Quinn and Rosie were.

"Take cover, Quinn," he yelled while pulling his gun from its holster.

I dropped to the floor, cradling Anastasia in my arms as I watched the blood pool around her.

Thirty-One

Quinn

1 Day Ago

"I know I've missed work all week," I replied into the phone. "Unfortunately, there have been a handful of personal events that have transpired and won't allow me to come in at this time."

I paused to listen to my boss rant and complain on the other end of the line, knowing that he was pissed off that I was being so vague. Was I going to lose my job over this? Who knew. But I couldn't exactly come clean and tell him that I was hiding and trying to keep my daughter safe from whoever was trying to kidnap her and taking out everyone that my dead husband had worked with. If ever my faith was shaken in who I could trust at work, now was that moment.

"I will touch base with you on Monday," I confirmed. "Thank you."

I hung up the phone and set it on the bed next to me. After Anastasia was shot in Mike's apartment this morning, we had agreed that none of us were safe in the city anymore. I repacked the same duffle bag that I had just barely unpacked yesterday, added some first aid stuff, and made sure that I had plenty of medicine if Rosie spiked a fever again. Thankfully, she seemed to be on the mend this morning, which was one less thing to worry about.

Roman had a friend who owned a remote cabin just outside of the city that we could stay at. We made our way this morning, creating enough of a zig-zag pattern with changing trains and taking cabs that no one would be able to follow us without being noticed. We got there around eleven, and

Rosie and I settled in while Roman checked the perimeter to make sure everything was safe and secure.

I hated that everything was constantly so stressful that she had missed so much school this week. I could tell that she was feeling the weight of everything by how cranky she was getting. She needed her normal routine that she hadn't had in almost two weeks. I also hated that I didn't have anything with me to keep her entertained. No toys. No movies. Nothing. It wasn't like I could take her outside and let her play just in case someone did find us out here.

We weren't that far from Manhattan, only a few hours away in Carmel Hamlet, but it felt far enough to give us some time to stop and refocus our attention. Whoever was coming for Rosie was sending us a clear message by taking out almost everyone that Justin had worked with. It terrified me that Mike was still back in the city, the only person who had a connection to Justin who hadn't been shot yet. Roman and Mike agreed that there wouldn't be any communication between them while we were out here, just to make sure the calls weren't traced to where we were. On top of that, Roman's friend said that the cell service at the cabin was pretty spotty given the thick trees that surrounded it, so it would be hard to get calls in or out.

I wanted an update on Anastasia and, more importantly, Julia. I didn't believe for one second that she was innocent in this and had been attacked on her way to work. Everyone else had been shot but her. Unfortunately, we fled as quickly as possible so we could find safety and weren't there when the paramedics came for Anastasia. As far as anyone knew, we weren't there when it happened, and that's how it needed to stay.

Rosie sat on the couch, staring at the TV that I hadn't bothered to turn on. I knew that she was miserable, and so was I. I looked around the small room, looking for a board game or something to entertain us for a while. As I scanned the room, I noticed a camera up in the corner pointed directly at the couch where she was sitting.

I casually adjusted my shirt, making sure that my gun was still strapped to me and easily accessible.

"Hey, pumpkin, I'm going to check on Roman for a minute. Are you okay in here for a few?"

She nodded and kept staring at the TV. I turned it on, assuming that the channels would be static since there wasn't cell service but was pleasantly surprised when I found a DVD player sitting on the shelf below the TV. There were a handful of movies on a bookshelf next to the couch, so I scanned them quickly before popping in a kid-friendly option and setting the remote on the wooden coffee table.

I glanced back at her one last time before I opened the door and stepped outside. I walked around, checking for Roman while keeping my attention focused on the house as well as any movement. Finally, I heard footsteps coming from the back of the cabin and saw Roman as he approached with a branch in his hand.

"Everything okay?" he asked, moving the wood over the tire marks from the Uber that had dropped us off earlier. It was a ten-minute walk to reach a spot where we would have cell service again, so we agreed that it was best not to risk renting a car that could be traced to us and instead would request another Uber when we were ready to leave or if we needed to go somewhere.

"Did you know that there are cameras inside?" I nodded to the cabin, turning to make sure Rosie hadn't ventured outside.

"Rob said that he had a few up. One in the living room aimed at the couch and one in the kitchen at the front door. They're not on, but I can call and ask him to turn them on if we want him to."

"Do we need them on?"

"It's up to you. Rob does surveillance, and it might not hurt to have an extra set of eyes on the cabin while we sleep. He also has the perimeter set up with cameras that are on 24/7, so he would know if someone approached the cabin."

"But there wouldn't be any way to warn us," I muttered with disappointment.

"There's a landline for emergencies. If he saw someone on the cameras, he would call and check to see if we were expecting anyone. Most of the time, they're set off by animals."

I nodded, feeling a little more comfortable with the cameras inside. At least it was limited to the living room and kitchen. It was a small cabin with only one bedroom and one bathroom, both of which had bars on the windows, so I knew there was no need to have any in those rooms.

"All done," he said, tossing the stick behind the wooden bench against the wall by the front door. I turned to go back inside when he snaked a hand around my waist and turned me to face him.

"How are you doing, Quinn?" His eyes searched mine.

"I honestly don't know. This is all just too much. I feel like I should be at work, trying to solve this case, but I can't."

I rested my head against his chest and inhaled, feeling comforted by his scent. It wasn't much, but I would take whatever comfort I could get right now.

Thirty-Two

Roman

1 Day Ago

I checked in with Trevor for what felt like the hundredth time today. I hated missing work, and while I tried to make up some of the time I'd been home with Quinn this week, I knew he already had a lot on his plate with Max's wedding this weekend. He didn't complain about me being gone and assured me that they had everything covered. Jackson was turning out to be quite the lifesaver these past few weeks with all of the unexpected time off Trevor and I had taken.

I sat on the small loveseat across from the sofa that Quinn and Rosie were cuddled on, watching another Disney movie that Quinn had found. It was boring, to say the least, but I was relieved that we were safe for now. I leaned my head back and closed my eyes.

When I opened them again, I saw Quinn and Rosie in the kitchen, snickering when they looked over at me and tried not to laugh. I sat up and felt something wet on the side of my mouth, so I quickly wiped it away with the back of my hand. Apparently, I had fallen asleep and drooled like a freakin' buffoon.

I got up and stretched before heading to see what they were doing in the kitchen that was connected to the small living room.

"What are you two ladies up to?" I asked, leaning over Quinn's shoulder as she kneaded a dough ball on the counter.

"We are making pizza," she said with a huge smile.

I was glad that she had agreed to make a quick stop at the grocery store just outside of town before we got here. I didn't want us to be stuck without food or toiletries, especially since we had Rosie. I could go days without eating, but the thought of letting her go hungry or skip a meal put a vice clamp on my heart and wouldn't let up until I knew that she would be taken care of.

Quinn had browsed the aisles, looking for something specific, while Rosie and I added a few bits of junk food here and there to the cart. I knew that Quinn and Rosie used to make pizzas at home a lot before everything happened, so I assumed this was her way of making things feel normal again for Rosie.

"It smells delicious," I commented. "What can I help with?"

"Do you want to make the salad?" Quinn asked, eyebrows raised.

"Ugh, do we have to eat salad?" Rosie whined with a scrunched face.

"Yes. Veggies are good for you, and we've eaten way too much junk food lately." Quinn pinned her with a look before turning to me and pointing a finger in my direction.

"Hey, I'm not complaining," I laughed with my hands raised.

"Everything is in the fridge. I found a cutting board and knife and set them by the sink."

"Cool," I said with a genuine smile and then winked at Rosie when she made another disgusted face about the salad. "Just wait until you try my salad, you'll *love* it!"

"Does it have ice cream or cookies in it?" Quinn joked.

I stopped for a moment and pretended to think about it, which made Rosie giggle. I loved that sound and wanted to hear it forever. I tried to push away the hope that fluttered in my chest that someday I would get to have more of these moments with them.

A few seconds later, I made a sad face at Rosie and started pulling the vegetables out of the fridge. I checked with Quinn to see what she wanted in the salad and what was being saved for the pizza, then I got started. We all worked together happily making dinner and not thinking about the cloud of darkness that seemed to be always looming over us.

After we ate, I cleaned up the dishes while Quinn gave Rosie a bath. She took her phone with her, letting me know that she was going to let her play in the water for a while since she had been cooped up inside for so long. I was about to remind her that there wasn't good cell service here when I realized she wasn't used to being away from it. It had become like a safety net, and I didn't want to take it from her.

She held it up and shook it gently as if reading my mind.

"I have a couple of books that I downloaded a while ago and never got around to reading. Figured I'll have some time to get started."

I smiled, and she returned it, the weight on my shoulders always feeling lighter when her beautiful face lit up the world around me.

They gave me a few minutes to use the restroom before they went in and got Rosie situated. I finished cleaning up and sat down on the couch, relaxing for a few minutes. I thought about going outside to check the perimeter to make sure there weren't any new footprints or tire tracks but then remembered that Rob had cameras set up, and if he had seen anything, he would have called.

He had also told me where the monitor was in the cabin that would show the live view of the cameras. I got up and opened the cabinet door, finding it exactly where he said it would be. The screen was large, with eight different cameras currently showing. The living room and kitchen cameras showed offline like he said they would. I looked around at all of the settings, finding where to turn them on if we wanted to. I needed to talk to Quinn before I did that, but in the meantime, I turned up the volume for the notifications; that way, if anything set off the cameras outside, we would hear it.

They stayed in the bathroom for over an hour before they came out and Rosie was in her pajamas with a big towel wrapped around her wet hair.

"Did you have a fun bath?" I asked, smiling at how happy she looked.

She nodded.

"Mama said I look like a raisin," she giggled.

I laughed and smiled up at Quinn as she sat down on the couch and pulled Rosie over to her. She rubbed the towel around her hair before she took it off and set it to the side.

"You are the cutest raisin I've ever seen," she said before leaning in and kissing Rosie's cheek, making her laugh again.

I watched as Quinn combed through her hair, getting the tangles out before braiding it.

"Thankfully, it's hot enough that her hair will dry quickly, even in a braid. At least this way, we won't have a mess of tangles to comb through in the morning."

I wasn't sure what was going through her mind, but I could hear the hint of uncertainty in her voice about not knowing what to expect. It sucked, always having to be on the lookout and ready to run at any moment.

Rosie curled up on the couch and watched another movie while Quinn hung the towel in the bathroom. As she was heading back, I heard a ding, and my eyes darted to the cabinet with the monitor. I had closed it, so Rosie didn't get curious about it, but the alert meant something had set off one of the cameras. Or better yet—someone.

Thirty-Three

Quinn

11 Hours Ago

I had been restless and fidgety since the alert for the camera went off earlier. Roman and I watched the video over and over, making sure we didn't miss anything as a raccoon scampered by, trotting right in front of the door. While I had hoped to see someone, I knew that we wouldn't. That would be too easy, and my life right now was anything but easy.

There wasn't anything on the video that indicated that someone was out there, but deep down inside, I knew that they were close. I could feel it in my bones.

By three, I still hadn't been able to fall asleep but was glad that Roman was finally getting some rest. Rosie was tucked into the bed with him on one side and me on the other. Thankfully, it was a king-sized bed, and there was plenty of room without us literally being on top of each other.

His soft snores still filled the room as I stayed awake until five. By then, I was exhausted and felt my eyes start to flutter shut when Rosie rolled over and tugged on my hand.

"Hey, baby girl," I said, sounding more tired than I wanted to.

"I have to go to the bathroom," she whispered.

"Okay, let's go." I tried to stifle my groan as I rolled off the bed and waited for her to get up. Roman shuffled and turned over, checking to see what was happening.

"She needs the restroom," I explained quickly, guiding her through the small room with my hand on her lower back. "You can go back to sleep."

I went with her and waited for her to finish as I leaned against the wall and closed my eyes for a minute. The toilet flushed, then she washed her hands and finished up. I hoped that she was still tired and wanted to go back to bed, but when she sat down on the couch, I knew she was up for the day.

I turned the TV on and set the remote on the coffee table before scampering off to the kitchen to start a pot of coffee. A few minutes later, Roman came out of the bedroom, pulling a clean t-shirt over his head, giving me a quick glimpse of his rock-hard abs in the process.

"Hey, I've got Rosie. Why don't you try to get some sleep."

"I'm fine, but thank you," I lied, feeling like my body weighed a thousand pounds as I tossed another scoop of coffee into the filter. At this rate, we were going to run out before tomorrow.

"You haven't slept, Quinn. You need to be alert, and you can't do that if your body doesn't have the rest it needs. I'll make her breakfast, and we can watch a movie together."

"How do you know if I've slept?" I asked with one hand on my hip.

"Because I heard you tossing and turning all night when you weren't up looking out the window or coming out here to check the cameras."

I groaned and covered my eyes with my hand.

"I'm so sorry I kept you up. I thought I was being quiet."

"You were. But I'm a light sleeper and have been trained to be aware of my surroundings at all times—even while I sleep. Now go lay down and rest. I'll come get you if we need anything."

I tried to find a reason to fight him on it—mainly because I wasn't used to anyone taking care of things for me—but I had very little fight left in me. I went to the room and laid down, making sure that the door was open so I could hear if anything happened.

Within minutes of my head hitting the pillow, I was asleep.

Hours later, a loud thud startled me from my sleep, and I jolted out of bed, looking for the source of danger. It took a moment for my head to clear as I looked frantically around the room, trying to remember where I was. Then it occurred to me that I was in the cabin, and Roman was supposed to be watching Rosie.

I bolted out of the room into the living room as I quickly looked for her. The TV was turned off, and there was no sign of them anywhere. The bathroom door was open, so she wasn't in there, and the kitchen was empty as well. I flung open the front door, ready to take off into the woods to find her when I saw them sitting on the bench right outside the door.

My hand flew to my chest as I tried to slow my racing heart. Roman's eyebrows raised in concern as Rosie's head tilted to the side in confusion.

"What's wrong, mommy?"

"I heard a loud thump and couldn't find you guys."

"Sorry, we came outside for a few minutes to get some fresh air."

I nodded, not sure what to say. Part of me was angry that he had taken her outside without asking me, but then I also knew that it was ridiculous to be upset when they weren't even ten feet away from the door and that he could quickly get her inside safely if someone did come.

"I was feeling sad, so Roman thought it would be fun to come look at the clouds and talk to Daddy."

My heart skipped a beat as sadness overwhelmed me. I looked at him without saying anything and wondered what they had been talking about.

"When I lost my grandpa, I used to sit outside and watch the clouds. I knew he was in heaven and that only the clouds separated us, so I would pick my favorite cloud and pretend he was sitting on it as I talked to him."

I smiled and looked down at Rosie, my arms folded over my chest as if to protect my heart from leaping out of my chest.

"Which cloud did you pick?" I asked her.

"That one. It's small, but it's shaped like a heart, and I think Daddy would pick that one to tell us that he loves us."

I nodded, fighting back the tears that threatened to spill over.

"I told Daddy that I was sad because I miss him and that you seem really sad lately too. I know that he can't come back to see us, but I really wish I could hug him again. Your hugs make me feel better, and I bet Daddy's would too."

"His hugs were the best," I said, squatting beside her and holding her hand. I knew that she didn't remember much about her time with him since she was only one year old when he passed. I tried to tell her stories over the years about Justin and showed her the videos I had of him, but it would never be enough to replace her knowing him and having her own relationship with her father.

"I had a dream about Daddy last night," she said quietly, lowering her head and eyes away from me.

"You did? What was it about?" I squeezed her hand reassuringly, hoping it would give her the confidence to tell me about it.

She looked up at Roman, and he nodded. I tried to ignore the pang of jealousy that rushed through me that she had chosen to talk to him about it yet seemed so reluctant to talk to me. Since when did she keep things from me?

"Daddy was with the lady who brought me home the other day from the subway. They were hugging each other, and then they… kissed." She looked up at me with guilt on her face, and it broke my heart. "Then he left with her, and I kept calling to him, asking him to come back, and he wouldn't. I was really mad at him."

I swallowed down the mix of emotions that she had just brought up and tried to focus on how to respond to her.

"I'm sorry, pumpkin. Dreams can be hard to understand sometimes, but I can promise you that Daddy would never walk away from you. You meant everything in the world to him."

She nodded and wiped a tear from her eye as we heard a clap of thunder far off in the distance. Roman looked up at the sky as the clouds moved with the rush of wind and the blue turned an ominous shade of gray.

"We should get inside before the storm hits," he said, standing up and gently placing his hand on Rosie's back to guide her inside.

Once she was inside, he lingered by the door and whispered in my ear, "I wouldn't worry too much about the dream. We all know how wild our imagination can get."

I forced a smile but knew there was more to her dream than he knew.

Thirty-Four

Roman

2 Hours Ago

Quinn seemed to relax a little as the rain pounded on the roof while she curled up and watched a movie with Rosie. This was probably the most I've seen anyone sit and watch movies, but it wasn't like there were any other options. If it was just Quinn and me, there were plenty of ways that I could fill the time without watching TV, but Rosie was here, and that left few options for a five-year-old.

It was a little after two, but it felt like it was so much later since we got up at five. I was glad that Quinn slept for a few hours but wished she would have gotten a solid eight hours of sleep instead of five. But something was better than nothing, and she seemed to be more alert than she was before.

I had fixed Rosie lunch earlier but knew that Quinn hadn't eaten yet today. Restless and desperate for something to do, I got up and went to the kitchen to make something since I hadn't bothered to eat either. My stomach growled as I turned the bacon in the skillet and flipped the pancakes onto a plate. Who said there was a time limit on when you could eat breakfast?

"Hey Rosie, do you want some pancakes?" I called to her in the living room. Not that I had to yell or shout, given that they were sitting less than twenty feet away from me in the same room. But pulling her attention away from the hundreds of spotted dogs on the TV was another thing.

"No thanks," she replied happily, leaning forward as Quinn got up and joined me in the kitchen.

"I hope you're hungry," I said over my shoulder as she pressed her body against mine and slid a hand up and down my back.

"I'm starving. What can I help with?"

"Nothing, I'm just about done."

"Sorry, I just assumed you were fixing food for yourself, or I would have come in to help."

"You don't need to apologize," I laughed. "I enjoy cooking for you, Quinn. I wouldn't have let you help, even if you tried."

She blushed and glanced at Rosie, who was still focused on the madwoman screeching her tires on the TV as she chased down the puppies in her car.

We sat down at the small kitchen table and ate, not bothering to say anything while checking on Rosie every few minutes. It wasn't that there was any threat of danger, but more out of habit and that there wasn't much else to look at in the small space without having to stare at each other—and I knew that if I kept looking at Quinn, I was going to start thinking about all of the things that I *couldn't* do to her right now.

Once we were finished, she helped me with the dishes, despite my constant protests. We were just about done when the phone rang. A chill ran down my spine as we looked at each other, knowing that Rob would only call if something was wrong.

I tossed the towel onto the counter and rushed over to the phone. My grip was tight as I picked up the receiver and brought it to my ear.

"Hello."

"It's Rob. There's a bad storm heading your way."

I looked out the window and saw a bolt of lightning light up the trees as the thunder clapped overhead. It had been slowly coming down for a few hours but was definitely getting worse.

"Yeah, it's already coming down pretty hard."

"The weather can get ugly out there, so if the power goes out, there's a generator in the shed behind the house. Might not be a bad idea to get it set up before it gets too bad. Just wanted to let you know in case I can't get through on this line."

He talked me through where to find everything I needed in the shed and then guided me on where to find resources if we needed them. I didn't have to ask what he meant. We both knew why we were here, and Quinn and I weren't the first to use his makeshift safe house.

I hung up, feeling slightly relieved that nothing was amiss, though I couldn't shake the gnawing feeling that something wasn't right. There were a few things that I needed to take care of before the power went out, so we weren't caught in a bind, but I knew that getting the generator set up was the first priority.

182

Thirty-Five

Quinn

The front door swung open, the rain spraying in from the wind that whipped past. I turned my head, knowing that Roman was back from messing with the generator but felt my body stiffen when I saw five figures dressed in all black, wearing ski masks, rush through the door.

I jumped off the couch, startling Rosie as I tried to shield her with my body. I reached behind for my gun, panic crushing over me when I remembered it wasn't there. It was unlike me not to have it on my body, but I had been distracted after I got out of the shower right before Roman went outside to prepare for the storm that was already upon us.

"NO!!" I shouted, shoving against the bodies as they charged us. I felt strong arms grab me and fling me to the side as Rosie screamed from the couch. I got up and swung at the masked figure in front of me, watching as their head shot to the side from the impact of my punch, but it wasn't enough. Someone held me by the waist, ensuring I couldn't get to Rosie.

Panic flooded through me as I tried to get free. It was useless, and I knew it. We were outnumbered and I was unarmed—biggest fucking mistake of my life.

I could hear Rosie scream and turned my head toward the sound right as someone picked her up and tossed her over their shoulder. A black pillowcase was shoved over her head as they rushed out the door. I continued to fight against the strong arms holding me in place, desperate to get to my daughter. My pulse raced and my breathing was erratic as adrenaline pumped through me.

I tried to turn to see where they had gone, the front door still wide open. There was a black van parked right outside that I immediately recognized. Seconds later, the back door was slammed shut before it sped off, the sound of gravel crunching beneath it.

I tossed my head back, feeling the sharp pain as I made contact with a head, eliciting a loud growl from the recipient. It wasn't enough to knock him out, but it did piss him off to where he tightened his grip around my throat, making it harder to breathe. I brought my hands up and tried to pry his hands away, desperate for air.

Roman will be back any second. He'll come save me. He'll take me to get Rosie back. Then we'll kick ass and take out everyone who's ever tried to hurt my daughter. She's only five years old...

But before Roman could get there, a hand reached up and covered my mouth with a towel. Everything turned black, and the voices around me faded.

Thirty-Six

Roman

My body felt like it had been electrocuted repeatedly. I laid on the ground, feeling the rain pelt my face as I tried to find the strength to roll over and get up.

I knew better than to come outside unarmed but hadn't expected to be ambushed when I went to turn on the generator. The storm was coming quickly, and Rob had warned me that we would likely lose power; unfortunately, I thought that we had more time than we did.

By the time I got outside to turn on the generator, the lights had already begun flickering in the house. I knew that it would only be a matter of minutes before we completely lost power and had asked Quinn to find the flashlights, candles, and matches that Rob had stored in the cabinet.

I looked around, checking for any signs of movement around me, though I knew they were already long gone. I heard them seconds before the first man approached me but wasn't quick enough before the second tasered and knocked me to the ground. While I had imagined they wanted to shoot me, I knew they didn't want to alert Quinn to their presence with gunfire. They needed the element of surprise on their side.

My body felt shaky as I forced myself to a sitting position. The rain was coming down even harder, making it impossible to see anything around me. With what little strength I had left, I pushed myself up and hustled back to the cabin. I wasn't sure how much time had passed, but I hoped I wasn't too late.

I rounded the corner and found the front door open and tire tracks in front of the door. I scanned the area, noticing another set that appeared bigger than the first. Knowing that they were already gone, I went inside and geared up to go find the two people who now meant more to me than anything in the world.

Once I was in dry clothes, I put on an armored vest and loaded it with extra mags, a flashlight, and a knife before holstering a 9mm to my thigh in addition to the AR15 slung across my back. Out of all of the things that I was thankful for with Rob, it wasn't the safe house that he had offered us but the gear that would allow me to do what I needed to do to get them back.

I had no idea where I would start looking for Quinn and Rosie, but I knew that I couldn't afford to waste another second. Time was of the essence right now, and their lives depended on me finding them before it was too late.

I walked down the road, following the tire tracks until I reached a spot where I had cell service. I knew that it would be a while before I could touch base with anyone, so I pulled out my phone and sent a quick text message to Trevor, letting him know that I would be taking an indefinite amount of time off from work.

A few minutes later, I heard my phone ding and checked it.

Trevor: Not a problem. Is everything okay?

Me: Quinn and Rosie are missing. I won't stop until I find them.

I turned my phone to silent and tucked it back into my pocket as I kept walking, following the tire tracks until they split at the fork in the road and went in two different directions.

Thirty-Seven

Rosie

"I have to use the bathroom." I squirmed on the seat and pressed my legs together as I hoped someone would take the dark bag off of my head. It was hot and gross inside of it, and I hated that I couldn't see anything. I wanted my mommy. Where was she?

There were voices whispering around me, sounding angry like the teachers when they go into the hallway to complain about the kids when they think no one can hear them. I always heard them, even when they thought they were being quiet. That's why I always tried to be good, so they wouldn't go talk about me.

Suddenly, I felt my body fall to the side before someone reached out to grab me. I had no idea who it was, but they didn't hurt me like the last person did. This time it was softer, like how my mom would hold my hand when we went to crowded places.

I tapped my feet as I tried to think about anything other than peeing. I didn't want to have an accident. Mommy said I was too old to have them and that the other kids would make fun of me if I had one. I wanted to wait until I could get to the restroom, but no one seemed to listen to me.

"I really need to go potty," I insisted to whoever could hear me.

Someone growled, and the sound was deep, like my Uncle Mike when he was fighting with my mom or grandma. But I didn't think it was him because why would he cover my head and not talk to me?

Suddenly, I was picked up and put over what I thought was someone's shoulder. It was difficult to tell, but it was hard and bony, and I could hear their loud breath by my ear.

Don't pee on them! They'll make fun of you and tell your mom that you had an accident. She'll be really mad at you.

I tried to squeeze my legs shut tighter to keep any pee from leaking out of me when I was plopped onto the floor and the bag on my head was ripped off.

I looked around, letting my eyes adjust to the bright light, trying to see where I was and who was with me when I felt a hand force my head in the other direction.

"Make it quick."

His voice was angry as he stormed off and left me in a bathroom with no windows. I was too afraid to look around so I kept my head down and walked over to the toilet.

My hands were shaky as I reached for my shorts and pulled them down. I looked up slightly, not seeing anyone around me before I sat down and went potty.

It was quiet, and I didn't know where the scary man had gone, but I was glad he wasn't there anymore.

I finished wiping, pulled my shorts and underwear back up, and then flushed the toilet. When I walked around the corner, I noticed a woman waiting for me by the sink, blocking the door.

My eyes widened, and a smile spread across my face.

"It's you! Did you find your puppy?" I asked, tilting my head to the side as I looked at my new friend. Then I remembered what my mom had told me. She wasn't my friend. She tried to take me from my grandma's house so she could kidnap me.

She didn't answer me. Come to think of it, she didn't look

happy to see me either. Was she upset about her puppy? Maybe she hadn't found it, and now I had made her sad. I turned on the water, squirted soap onto my hands, and started washing them.

"Are you here to help me?" I asked as I turned off the water.

I looked around for a dryer or a paper towel but stopped when I saw the sad smile on her face as she slowly shook her head no.

Thirty-Eight

Quinn

I laid completely still and pretended to be unconscious as the truck turned a corner down the bumpy, unpaved road. One thing that I learned early on was to remember as many details as possible. The FBI had ingrained that into us from the very beginning, and it had stuck with me since. Details could make the difference between solving a case and saving a life.

While I had lost consciousness for a few minutes—maybe longer, who knew—I had kept quiet once I came to and made sure I stayed in the position I was in when they loaded me into the vehicle. I needed every advantage that I could get at this point, and that meant that if I pretended to be unconscious, they would be more likely to slip and say something about where they were taking me or about who had Rosie.

I kept my breathing shallow and slowly lifted my eyes, making sure they were only partly open so I could look around without anyone seeing that I was awake. I was on my side in the backseat with my hands bound in front of me with thick rope. It felt like I was possibly taking up two seats, but I couldn't tell if anyone was on the other seat beside me. It was too risky to look over and check and even riskier to move my body which would alert them that I was either awake or slowly coming to.

First glance showed two men sitting up front with a middle console between them. Based on the size of the vehicle, I imagined it was a truck or SUV, and given the beat-up interior, I would guess that whoever had Rosie wasn't rolling in money. Either that or they hired their goons and didn't bother to outfit them with expensive, bullet-proof vehicles like those in the mafia had.

I tucked my chin to my chest as slowly as possible and held my breath. So far, no one seemed to notice any movement on my end so I tilted my head a fraction of an inch until I could see the seat beside me.

Sure enough, there was a man sitting next to me, wearing all black just like the other two up front, with a ski mask covering his face. I hated that none of them were stupid enough to take the masks off; it would make it a whole lot easier for me if I knew who they were.

I continued to study him as he held onto the handlebar above his window and stared out the window. There was a .45 in his shoulder holster, and I knew it was likely he had other weapons that I couldn't see, as well as the two guys sitting up front. I slowly pulled my head back and rested it on the seat while I waited for us to get wherever we were going. My body had already been through plenty, combined with a lack of sleep, so I needed to preserve energy any way I could.

Given that I had no idea where we were headed, I was desperate to come up with a plan of attack for when we got there. If I wanted to keep Rosie alive, I needed to get to her as soon as possible. However, I also couldn't stop wondering if Roman was okay and whether he had made it back to the cabin. I hadn't heard any gunshots before the intruders burst through the door, but that didn't mean they didn't use a suppressor to cover the sound. With the wind and rain that pelted against the cabin, it wouldn't take much to muffle it. Not knowing anything about either of them weighed too heavily on my mind and I needed to focus, or I wouldn't be of any help to anyone.

I hated that I had no idea how much time had passed, but it was even worse that I was separated from Rosie and didn't know if she was still alive. I prayed that she was, but I just couldn't stop the pain in my heart at the thought that something had happened to her. If Justin weren't already dead, I would kill him for putting us in this situation to begin with.

My breathing was calm and even, not giving it away that I was awake. I felt movement beside me and forced my eyes closed while I held my breath and waited for him to shift his position.

"Boss said to go the back way," a gruff voice said, breaking the silence in the cab.

"Got it."

It felt like the vehicle was slowing down, but I didn't trust that it was safe to open my eyes just yet. Was I supposed to still be knocked out? How much time had passed before they would just assume that I was dead? I had no clue but decided to go along with my instincts and allowed my body to appear lifeless on the seat as the car stopped.

Here we go.

Thirty-Nine

Roman

My head was still pounding as I trekked through the thick forest, trying not to lose sight of the tire tracks on the dirt road. I took a few seconds to decide which way to go once I had come to the fork but didn't have the luxury of taking any longer than that. Thankfully the rain was slowing down, but I knew I had to hurry before they washed away and I was left with nothing.

I had limited cell service as I walked and was thankful that I had been able to get a text message out to Trevor. I wanted to track Quinn's Apple watch, but that would have cost more time while I waited for the signal to be strong enough to find it, and I simply didn't have time to spare.

It irritated me that I didn't know which vehicle Quinn was in compared to which one had Rosie, but I went with my instincts and chose the bigger tracks. Maybe it was because I knew that they would be easier to track and less likely to fade right away with the weather. Or maybe it was simply that I assumed Rosie was in this vehicle. I knew that Quinn had a better chance of protecting herself and that she would fight like hell to get to her daughter. Rosie, on the other hand, was only five years old and needed all of the help she could get.

I pushed harder every time I felt like slowing down and resting. I had no idea how long I'd been walking, but I did know that there wasn't time to stop now. I looked around for any sign of a building or house but didn't see anything. It didn't matter. I would walk a thousand miles with bloody feet and no food to get to her. Nothing was going to stop me now.

Suddenly the rain started pouring with a vengeance while thunder clapped off in the distance. Apparently, this wasn't going to be as easy as I had hoped. Not that any of it was easy—but I didn't really need any additional complications at this point.

I stopped for a second, took a deep breath, and reminded myself that I had survived worse. I had served in the Marines. I was used to hiding in the shadows and taking the lives of those who least expected it. There wasn't anything that I couldn't do.

Memories of years of stakeouts played through my mind as I continued walking, images I had long since tried to erase from my mind. I reminded myself that I wasn't that person anymore. I was different now. I wasn't a heartless killing machine like I thought I was when I first returned from my last tour. And while I wasn't proud of what I had done, I knew that I would do all of it again in a heartbeat because I had helped rid the world of some of the worst scum it had ever seen.

Even though I wasn't in combat and taking orders, I knew that I was doing the world another favor by eliminating whoever had taken Rosie. There were plenty of sick perverts that would continue to lurk in the shadows and prey on innocent children, but I would be damned if they touched her.

I stopped and ducked behind a large, overgrown tree when I spotted an abandoned-looking cabin in the distance. Parked out front was an older, beat-up truck that had seen better days. Fresh mud was splashed up on the doors, so I knew it was the tracks I had been following. That was helpful, given that the rain was really coming down hard now and already starting to erase them.

Keeping myself hidden behind the tree, I scanned the area and took note of how many entrances there were into the building. I was relieved that I hadn't spotted any other vehicles, but there was a detached garage off to the side, which meant there could be more occupants inside.

The paint was peeling on the front door and the windows were boarded up, making it impossible to see inside. I chewed the inside of my cheek in frustration, knowing that I needed to have a calculated plan before I entered. Rosie's safety depended on it.

I looked around, making sure no one was guarding the perimeter, then inched my way closer to the house while staying in the shadows. If I couldn't see in the house, then hopefully, I would be able to hide outside and listen to what was happening inside. I quickly circled around the cabin with my 9mm drawn and aimed in front of me as I made sure no one was out here with me. Once it was clear, I found a spot beside one of the side windows and squatted beside it.

The blood rushed through my ears, making it hard to make out the faint voices from inside. I knew it would take a few minutes for my pulse to return to normal, but I didn't have that much time to wait. I stood up and leaned closer, resting my ear against the brittle wood, and prayed that it was firmly secured so I didn't risk exposing myself.

"How long has she been out?" a man's voice asked.

"Who knows," someone muttered, sounding further away and less interested.

"The order is to deal with her."

"So then do it."

"Have you checked the account? Has the money been posted?" It was hard to tell how many different voices I was hearing, but this one sounded the same as the first man who spoke, the baritone in his voice recognizable compared to the other voice.

"Not yet," another voice answered. Instinctively I pulled away when it sounded like they were on the other side of the wall from me.

"Then she lives until we get paid," the first man stated.

"But that's not the order."

"I don't give a fuck what the order is. They hired us to do a job, and I'm not doing it until we have that money. There's too much at stake to be fucking around with these lunatics. Get an update on when they're transferring the funds. Until then—she stays alive."

<u>Forty</u>

Quinn

I sat in a chair by the window with my hands still tied in front of me. I couldn't pretend to be unconscious anymore, especially after one of them had kicked me in the ribs and I groaned in response. Now that I was awake, they were discussing what to do with me. It was apparent that I wasn't supposed to live long enough for them to bother with tying me to the chair, which was stupid on their part.

To add to their stupidity, all three of the men now had their ski masks off, allowing me to memorize every detail of their hideous faces. From the tattoos that covered the tall one's face to his neck to the one with no teeth and a receding hairline—they weren't anyone that I had seen before in any of the cases that I'd worked. Toss in the fact that they were discussing how to get rid of me, and I knew that they were simply hitmen for hire and not at all associated with whoever had Rosie.

My Rosie. My heart ached at the thought of my sweet girl somewhere alone with these monsters and I prayed that she was okay. *Had Roman gotten to her? Was he okay?*

I subtly shook my head to clear it and focused on the task at hand.

While they were busy talking, I scanned the room for anything I could use to my advantage. My hands were still tied and I didn't have a weapon on me, which meant that I would have to rely on improvising.

Two of the men wore shoulder holsters but didn't appear to have any armor on. The third guy didn't have armor on, nor did he appear to have a weapon. He was short and stocky with a gut that begged to be punched. I looked between them, searching for anything that would tell me who would be the hardest to take down—that's where I would start.

"I don't care what they said. I want the money, and I want it now," the short guy sneered into the phone.

The guy with the tattoos rolled his head on his neck, closing his eyes briefly while he did. Out of the three of them, he was the largest and most muscular. The other guy had a few missing teeth, but other than that, he wasn't in that bad of shape. If I had to choose between the two of them—and I did—I knew that the one with the tats would be my biggest challenge.

As if lady luck was on my side, the short guy on the phone turned and paced by the boarded-up window next to the front door and continued to tap the screen of his phone. No Teeth Tom, as I decided to name him, took off down the hall after announcing he was taking a piss.

That left Tatted Tim and me. He rolled his neck again, and I took that moment to make my move. Within seconds, I jumped up from the chair, ducked to avoid his hand that reached out to grab me, and slid down as if I was trying to steal home base. As I was mid-slide, I swung my hands up and punched him in the balls. It was difficult with my hands tied, but I knew it was the only way to disable him quickly.

As he hunched over in pain, I spun around and grabbed the .45 from his holster. Without giving it a second thought, I pulled the trigger and sent a bullet straight through his head. His body hit the floor at the same time the short one came rushing over. Before he could reach me, I put a bullet through his chest and then another one in his head, just to be sure.

Now that two out of the three were eliminated, there was one left, and I prayed that he would be talkative after seeing his two buddies. I needed at least one of them to give me information on where Rosie was and who was paying them to kill me. I waited with my hands steady in front of me for him to come back from the bathroom. I didn't imagine he was in any rush, given that he likely assumed those bullets were for me and that the job was done.

A few minutes later, I heard the bathroom door open, and heavy footsteps headed toward me from the hallway. Before they got there, the front door burst open. I spun around, aimed, and fired.

Forty-One

Roman

I jumped to the side as a bullet whipped past me. My heart jumped into my chest when I saw Quinn standing there with a gun aimed at me. I was thankful that I had been able to dodge it but also incredibly impressed with how accurate her aim was in the first place.

After I heard the first gunshot, I knew that I had no choice but to get inside. Little did I know that it was her in here and not Rosie.

"It's me, Quinn," I announced loudly, even though she could clearly see me.

I didn't bother to look at her as I kept my focus on the man walking into the room. His eyes widened as he saw the two bodies bleeding out on the wood floor, then narrowed as he looked between Quinn and me. Before he could reach his hand up to grab his gun, I raised mine and held it steady in front of me.

"Don't even think about it," I said, using my foot to kick the door shut behind me.

Quinn blinked a few times as if she couldn't believe I was there.

"Quinn, step aside," I directed, moving in closer to the guy as I watched his fingers twitch at his sides. I knew he would make a move to grab his gun, and I couldn't afford for Quinn to get caught in the middle.

She moved a few steps away from me and turned her aim to him. I knew she was focused again as I made it the last few feet and stood in front of him.

"Make one move, and I will put a bullet through your brain, just like my girl here did to your friends. Got it?"

He nodded, his glare as cold as ice.

I quickly relieved him of the guns in his shoulder holster before patting him down and removing a knife from his waistband. Once I was confident that he was no longer a threat, I stepped back and aimed the AR15 at his head.

"Go sit on the couch."

He didn't say anything and did as he was told.

Quinn was still standing there, holding her gun steady with both hands bound together. I wanted to cut her free but didn't trust that he wouldn't do something while we were distracted. She seemed comfortable enough, given that she had already killed two men while bound.

He dropped down onto the couch and then looked between us with his brows raised.

"Let's just cut to the chase," I said, widening my feet as I kept my aim. "Who do you work for?"

He rolled his eyes and looked away.

I clenched my teeth and stared him down. If he wanted to play games and pretend to be a tough guy, that was fine. We would see just how tough he was.

I glanced at Quinn and caught her eye for a brief second, nodding in his direction. She gave a subtle nod and kept her hands steady in front of her.

I returned my attention to him, picked a spot on the wall half an inch above his head, and fired.

He jumped up, his head whipping around to see the hole in the wall.

"That was the only warning shot you're going to get." I adjusted my aim, making sure he knew that it was now focused on the spot right between his eyes. "Start talking."

"I don't know anything," he stammered, looking from me to Quinn as his eyes softened.

"Stop looking at her like that," I snapped. "She's not going to pity you, dumb ass. You helped them kidnap her daughter; there's no way you're getting out of this alive."

"Tell us what you know," she said coldly, lifting her hands slightly as she reminded him that she wasn't interested.

"As I said, I don't know anything. My boss—the guy with the bullets in him," he nodded to the short guy, "he handled everything. We just did what we were told."

"What were you told?" I asked, pulling his attention back to me.

"Take her out, and we would get $50,000."

I raised my brows and glanced at Quinn. She frowned angrily, and I had to bite back a laugh. She was worth more than that, and we both knew it.

"What about the little girl?" I pushed. We didn't care about how much they were getting for killing Quinn. We needed to know where Rosie was and what the price tag was for her.

"I don't know. I wasn't told anything about her."

"Alright, what happens after you complete this job?" Quinn asked.

"We were waiting for the money. Once we had that, we were supposed to take care of the job and send them proof."

"Send who proof?" I yelled, getting frustrated quickly.

"I. Don't. Know." He enunciated each word as if I were stupid and then turned to Quinn. "He doesn't listen for shit, does he?"

She cocked her head to the side and then raised the .45 slightly before putting a hole in the wall next to mine. I smiled proudly at how accurate her shot was. It wasn't the time to think about it, but suddenly I was imagining dates with us at the shooting range, seeing who could beat who.

"Fuckin bitch!" he shouted and jumped up from the couch.

"Sit your ass down before I put a bullet in it," I demanded.

"As you can see, we both have *remarkable* aims. I would stop fucking around and tell us what we're asking because I can *guarantee* you that if you don't tell me what I need to know, I will put as many bullets in your body as it takes until I'm no longer pissed off. And right now—I'm fucking furious," Quinn warned.

He sighed and returned to the couch, suddenly looking defeated.

"I don't know their names. My boss was handling it. If you want info, I would check his phone. He was supposed to send a picture, you know, *proof* that it was done."

I looked around for the phone, then spotted it a few feet away on the floor, sticking out from under his arm. I nodded to Quinn, suggesting that she be the one to get it. Between both of us, I had no doubt that she could take him out if needed, but since her hands were still bound, I figured she might need the break.

She returned my nod, lowered her gun to the table beside me, then bent down to pick up the phone. I watched her through peripheral vision while I kept my eyes on him.

I could tell that she hadn't dealt with many dead bodies as she nervously tried to figure out a way to retrieve the phone without touching him. Finally, she grabbed the end of it and pulled it out.

"It's locked," she muttered, looking up at me under her thick lashes.

"Does it need a pin or a thumbprint?"

She swiped her fingers across the screen, a look of determination on her face. Then she bent down, lifted the dead guy's thumb, and tried not to gag as she pressed it against the phone.

It took a couple of tries before she got the angle right. Once it was unlocked, she dropped his hand and stood up, scanning the recent call log and text messages.

"There aren't any names in here." She looked helplessly at me. "It's all code."

"What are the codes?"

"Red," she said and then looked at the guy on the couch. "What does red mean?" She held the phone in the air and shook it at him.

He shrugged and looked away.

Before the phone could lock again, she started looking through it and then gasped. Her eyes filled with tears as she stared at whatever was on the screen.

"What is it, Quinn?"

She turned the phone toward me. On the screen was a photo of Mike.

"Why is there a picture of your brother on his phone?" I asked, furrowing my brow.

Before Quinn could answer, the asshole on the couch decided to speak up.

"Because he's the next assignment. The payout increases the sooner we deliver him."

"We have to stop them," Quinn whispered.

"It's too late for that," he snorted. "They sent a sniper in this morning."

Forty-Two

Rosie

"I don't like bologna," I said as the mean man shoved a sandwich at me. I kept my hands tucked under my butt so I didn't have to take it.

"Then go hungry." His nose flared the same way Uncle Mike's does when he gets mad. I pulled away, afraid that he might hurt me.

"How long before they get here?"

I looked up at the woman who was yelling into her phone. She looked familiar, but I didn't know why. I tried to hide against the wall and make myself as small as possible on the chair so she wouldn't see me. She was mad. Really really mad. I didn't want her to get mad at me again.

"What do you mean that they're *gone?* Your guys had one job. ONE. JOB."

She stopped walking around and I was thankful because her shoes were really loud and hurt my ears every time they clicked on the floor. Mommy's shoes sounded like that when she wore her high heels, but she didn't do that too much anymore. She said she was too tired to worry about running around in death traps. I didn't know what she meant by it, but I thought maybe they made this lady mad too. Perhaps she could take them off for a while, or someone could loan her a pair of shoes that she liked better? That might make her less angry.

"So what you're telling me is that not only did your team let them get away, but they killed them first, then stole the truck AND Paco's phone?"

The louder she yelled, the more I thought about asking someone to give her different shoes. She started walking again and pinched her nose. Mommy also did that when she had a headache. Maybe something was wrong with her and she needed help. I looked around for a nurse or someone that could help her. Everyone else looked scared or mean, so I didn't want to talk to any of them. I shuffled in my seat and tried to make myself invisible again.

"Well, given that your team botched the first job, you're obviously not getting paid. What's the status of the other assignment?"

The mean guy with the gross sandwich walked by again and looked at me but didn't stop, so I knew I must have finally turned invisible. It was something that I used when I went places with mommy and didn't want people to see me. I didn't know if it really worked until now. I couldn't wait to tell her about it later.

"Well, at least you guys got half of the job done. I want proof sent to me in ten minutes. After that, find the other two and deal with them."

She hung up the phone and turned around to look at me.

I panicked, wondering if my invisibility had worn off or if she had special powers like Mommy and could see me.

I held my breath and grabbed the seat of the chair tightly as she walked over and squatted in front of me.

"When someone offers you food, you should take it. You never know when it might be your last bite to eat."

She stood up, grabbed the sandwich from the mean guy, and shoved it at me. When I didn't take it from her right away, she got really angry and shook it in front of me.

"Take it!" she screamed at me, jerking her head so hard that her red hair looked like fire on top of her head.

I reached up and took the sandwich.

"Good girl." She smiled at me but it didn't make her eyes sparkle like my moms did when she smiled at me.

Forty-Three

Quinn

"There's still no answer," I sighed, listening as Mike's phone went to voicemail.

We were in the truck we stole after killing the last guy in the cabin. Not only did we take the truck, but we also loaded up on weapons and stripped them of anything useful, including the phone they had been using to keep in contact with whoever had Rosie.

As soon as we had a signal, Roman reached out to a friend and had them start tracking the number programmed in the phone under Red. While he drove, I focused on calling Mike and watching the other phone to see if anyone called or texted with an update on the assignments their team was supposed to complete.

"Trevor said that he and Max were headed over to go look for him."

I hated all of the unknown and wished that all of this was over with already.

A text message alert came through on the other phone, and I immediately put in the password I had changed it to and unlocked it.

Roman glanced over to see what it was, but my excitement was quickly replaced with frustration when I opened the message.

"I swear, this guy gets more naked pictures sent to him than anyone I know. And honestly, he's not attractive enough to generate this much attention from women," I complained and exited out of the message.

"Looks has nothing to do with it," Roman laughed. "You know when you have access to drugs and money, women will do anything to get to it."

"I know. But it's still disgusting." I scrunched my face.

"It's true. Some women will do anything for a little taste of that life."

I leaned my head back on the seat and closed my eyes, hoping that some sort of divine intervention would happen and guide me to where Rosie was.

"We're going to find her," Roman assured me for the hundredth time since we'd gotten into the truck.

"It's been hours. Anything could have happened by now."

"Stop thinking like that, Quinn. You have to stay positive."

"I know," I groaned and blew out an irritated breath. I turned and looked out the window.

Roman's phone started ringing and I whipped my head in his direction as he answered it on speaker phone.

"Hey man," he said loudly. "Have you found him?'

There was a loud sigh—the kind you hear when someone's about to give you bad news and they don't want to.

"We have him."

"What does that mean?" I blurted out, needing more information.

"It means no line is secure right now, so I can't say more than that."

"Trevor!" I yelled, turning in my seat to face Roman. I was starting to lose it and there was no stopping me. I had reached a breaking point, and not knowing whether my brother was dead or alive was enough to snap the final straw.

"Thanks for the update," Roman said, eyeing me cautiously while also keeping an eye on the road.

"No problem. I'll be out of town for a bit and won't have constant access to my cell. Service is kinda spotty out there."

"Gotcha. Thank you."

I stared at Roman in disbelief as he ended the call and stared straight ahead.

"What the fuck was that code for?!" I shrieked.

"They have him, Quinn. That's all they're going to tell us right now."

"How can you be so calm about it? We don't know if he's alive or dead or in need of medical attention!"

He reached over and squeezed my hand gently.

"Trevor is going out of town, which means that Mike is alive and they're hiding him. He's with Max, and the two of them know plenty of doctors that will treat Mike without it being on anyone's radar."

"How do you know this?"

He shrugged and looked out the window, avoiding me.

"Roman."

"Look, I can't get into details but trust me when I say that Mike is in good hands. I hate not knowing if he's okay, but I trust Trevor and Max. If he says that they've got him, they've got him. There's nothing more that we can do, Quinn. Right now, we need to trust them to take care of Mike so we can focus on Rosie."

I let my head fall back and closed my eyes.

"You're right. I'm sorry." My shoulders were so tight that

they felt permanently attached to my ears.

"You don't need to be sorry. All of this is beyond stressful, and I get it. But we're a team, and that means that we all help each other when needed."

I felt my heart start to slow back down to a normal pace and focused on taking some deep, grounding breaths. I had to get my mind clear if I wanted to figure out where Rosie was.

"Have you found anything else in the phone?" he asked, nodding to it sitting in my lap.

I shook my head and picked it up.

"I haven't been able to figure out the code. Red could mean anything, and other than dirty texts from countless women, there isn't anything about other assignments, so it's not like I can compare them to see if there's a theme of some sort."

"Maybe we should call Red? See if they answer?"

I pulled my mouth to the side as I thought about it.

"It couldn't hurt…."

I unlocked the phone and found the name Red in the contacts, which was fairly easy given there weren't many names, to begin with. I pressed the call button and put it on speakerphone so Roman could hear it.

We waited quietly as it rang. By the fifth ring, I was already feeling disappointed that they wouldn't answer.

"Since I've been informed that the men I hired are all dead and were left abandoned in an empty cabin without their weapons, I'm going to guess this is Quinn."

My stomach dropped as I stared at the phone. Roman nodded for me to answer her.

"Where is my daughter," I demanded, my fingers trembling

as I struggled to hold the phone.

"Oh, sweet Rosie? She's fine. She's right here with me, getting to know everyone as we get her settled in. She's quite beautiful, isn't she?"

"You fucking bitch!" I shouted, blinded by anger. "Tell me where my daughter is now!"

"Tsk, tsk. Always such a hot head."

I looked to Roman for help, but his focus was on the road ahead of him as his knuckles turned white from gripping the steering wheel.

"How do you know that I'm a hot head?" I asked, forcing myself to calm down. It wouldn't do any good to sit here and yell at her. I needed to focus on finding Rosie, which meant that I had to get her to tell me where she was.

"I know everything there is to know about you, Quinn. I've been studying you for a long time. And quite frankly, I've always thought that Justin could do better."

My nostrils flared as my face twisted with anger.

"She's just trying to get to you; ignore her," Roman whispered.

"Well, then, you won't mind me stopping by to say hi," I replied as coolly as I could.

"Unfortunately, we aren't up for visitors right now. It seems *sweet* little Rosie isn't feeling the best, so I need to tend to her. Make sure she's *ready*. But feel free to come say hi to my guards. They've been searching for you, so this would make their job that much easier."

I glanced over to find Roman on his phone, speaking quietly into it.

"I don't think so," I snorted. "I am coming for my daughter;

come hell or high water. As you've already seen—your men don't stand a chance with me. Now tell me where she's at."

"Don't you get it, Quinn? I already have what I want. What I've wanted for years. Now it's just a simple matter of tying up loose ends and cleaning up the mess your husband started."

"What does Justin have to do with this?" I asked, trying to keep her on the phone while Roman talked on his.

"He ruined my life," she shouted, forcing me to pull away. "He. Ruined. Everything. And now it's time to make it right. To fix what he tried to destroy."

Before I could say anything more, the line went dead.

I tossed the phone on the dashboard in frustration and scrubbed my hands down my face.

"Don't worry, I know where they're at," Roman assured me.

I didn't stop to think about what he said because my mind was too busy and distracted trying to place her voice. It was familiar. I had heard it before.

The wheels in my head were turning rapidly when it suddenly clicked into place.

"It's Julia. She has Rosie."

Forty-Four

Roman

"Okay, it should be right over there," I said, nodding to a small clearing in between the thick forest in front of us.

"So, what's the plan?" Quinn asked, already taking her seat belt off.

I parked the truck on the side of the road, hiding it the best I could, given the size of the damn thing. Then, I turned the ignition off and turned to face her.

"We wait a few minutes; make sure it's safe before we head in."

Her brows shot up off her forehead as her eyes bulged out.

"Are you kidding me? You think my daughter is in there, and you want me to wait to make sure it's safe?! Nothing is safe with her in there right now, Roman!" She turned and reached for the handle as my hand darted across to stop her.

"I don't want to wait either, Quinn, but what choice do we have? We have to be smart about this, which means we can't just rush in with guns blazing. This isn't some cheesy action flick. It's real life, and your daughter's life is at stake. I'm not willing to jeopardize that. We have no idea how many people are inside and what we're facing once we get there. I would hate for them to put a bullet through our heads before we even make it to the door. They likely have cameras set up around the property which means they're going to see us long before we see them. We're already at a disadvantage; let's not make things harder than they already are."

She sunk back against the seat and sighed heavily.

"Fine, you're right."

I knew how she felt because I was just as frustrated that we couldn't rush in and get Rosie but serving twelve years in the Marines taught me that you didn't go in unless you knew what was waiting on the other side. Intelligence was vital, and even though we didn't have time to get all of the information we needed, we had to be smart enough to get the basics.

Ten minutes felt like hours as we sat and waited to see if any cars would come or go from the road that we needed to head down. A no trespassing sign was posted at the entrance, so I didn't expect much traffic other than those we needed to avoid.

We got out of the truck and watched our surroundings for any movement as we geared up. Quinn had taken one of the shoulder harnesses from the cabin before we left and now had it loaded with extra ammo in addition to the .45 and 9mm she had swiped from the dead guys. I adjusted the tactical vest and made sure it was in place before leading the way with my AR15 aimed ahead of me.

Quietly, we stalked through the tall grass, making sure to keep off of the road and stay hidden under the thick trees. We had no idea if they had cameras set up or if they had a team stationed outside, but we would soon find out.

I didn't have to glance behind me to make sure Quinn was still there. Her soft footsteps were the steady reminder that I needed to push forward. I knew that she wanted to take off and run to get her daughter and that it was taking everything inside of her not to. Hell, it was taking everything I had not to do it either.

Finally, the road beside us opened into a large gravel driveway in front of a massive house. There were several cars parked outside, but none that I recognized. We stopped and studied the house, looking for any signs of movement around it.

When we knew it was safe, we slowly moved forward, making sure to stay hidden. We approached the side of the house, and I took my spot at the front of the wall while Quinn trailed around to the back, clearing it before she joined me.

There was an open window above us on the second story of the house, but it was small and likely belonged to a bathroom, given the size. I looked around for other points of entry, frustrated that there weren't any windows or doors nearby.

What kind of people build a house without windows or doors? How creepy and depressing is that?

The kind of people who kidnap and traffic children.

I was about to tell Quinn that we should circle around to the other side when we suddenly heard a voice and froze.

"But I don't want to," Rosie said grumpily.

"I don't care if you want to. You will learn to do as you're told."

I felt my blood pressure rise, knowing that Quinn's was too.

"I just want my mommy."

"Well, lucky for you, I'm your mommy now."

Forty-Five

Rosie

My face felt gross after the tears stuck to it. I asked for a tissue, but the mean lady told me that I wasn't allowed to cry and that maybe this would teach me not to do it again.

I didn't like the house we were in. She kept saying it was home, but it didn't feel like it. There were no pictures on the walls. No windows to look outside. There wasn't even a fireplace for Santa to come down. Nothing about it felt like my home.

I missed my mommy. I wanted to see and hug her, but the mean lady got mad whenever I talked about my real mom. She said she's my mom now, but that's not true either. Just like my mom always told me that no one would ever replace my real dad, I knew that the mean lady was lying and that no one would replace my real mom.

She left me alone in a room and told me to get used to it because it would be my new room. There wasn't anything in it other than a bed and a toy box that didn't have any toys. I hated it already.

I sat on the bed and pouted until the door opened.

"Can I come in?"

"No," I muttered. I didn't like this girl either. She lied to me about being my friend and needing my help to find her puppy.

She didn't listen and came in anyway. When she closed the door behind her, I felt scared, but then she smiled, and it didn't feel as scary anymore.

"You have to be very quiet, okay, Rosie? Julia doesn't know I'm in here," she said softly, the way my mom talks to me when she's trying not to be too loud.

I nodded and watched her sit on the edge of the bed.

"We don't have much time before they come looking for me, but I wanted to talk to you about something. Okay?"

I nodded again.

"Has your mommy ever taught you what to do if a stranger tried to hurt you?"

This time I was afraid to nod, so I just sat there quietly on the bed.

"Do you know what to do, Rosie?"

I shrugged my shoulders. Mommy had told me lots of stuff, and then Uncle Mike and Roman had taught me how to fight off the bad guys recently, but they said I shouldn't tell anyone about it.

"If anyone tries to touch you, I want you to do what your mommy told you to do. Okay?"

I chewed my bottom lip and debated on whether I should tell her that I knew how to fight off the bad guys.

"It's okay," she continued. "You can tell me whatever you want to. I'm not here to hurt you, Rosie."

My breath felt funny in my lungs as I tried to talk.

"Uncle Mike and Roman taught me how to fight, but they told me not to tell anyone because Mommy might get mad." I lowered my head as if I were already in trouble for saying it.

"What did they teach you?"

I leaned forward and showed her some of the punches I had learned.

"Just like that," I said, getting up and standing in front of her to show her the rest.

"That's great, Rosie," she smiled. "I want you to use those moves they taught you, okay? If anyone tries to touch you, you fight them just like your uncles showed you."

I nodded and felt my cheeks burning from the smile that stretched across them.

"I have to go but promise me that you'll use what you showed me. Okay?"

"Okay."

Before she left, I decided to ask her one more question.

"Why did you lie to me about losing your puppy?"

Her face fell into sadness as she thought about it.

"Because it was my job. I was told to do it." She took a deep breath and then let it out. "I didn't have a choice."

"Why didn't you just say no?"

"They don't like it when you say no. That's why I want you to promise me that you'll fight with everything you have inside of you."

"Did you have to fight them too?"

"No," she said quietly as tears formed in her eyes. "No one ever taught me to. My mom wasn't here to help me, and I didn't know what to do. That's how I got stuck here, in this life."

"Do you think I'll ever see my mommy again?" I asked, my lip trembling as I started to cry.

"I don't know. I really hope so."

She opened the door and left me alone in the room that still didn't feel like home.

Forty-Six

Roman

Hearing Rosie's voice was enough to get both of us moving quickly as we circled to the other side of the house. I led the way with my AR15 and was ready to fire.

The trees were thick around the back of the house, allowing us plenty of room to hide if needed. While I knew that we were likely being watched on camera anyway, I knew that a bullet was more likely to be stopped by a thick tree trunk than thin air, so I took comfort in the resources around us.

Quinn followed closely behind me, her steps almost perfectly in time with mine. I pushed out the flashbacks of being a Marine and stayed focused on the present. I wasn't in combat, and this wasn't a team effort. This was me by myself, trying to save the woman I loved and her daughter.

About fifteen feet ahead of us, there was movement by a large, overgrown tree. I quickly raised my hand, signaling Quinn to stop. I held my breath as I listened for more. A twig snapped beneath their weight as they stepped over it, the loud thud of their boots echoing around us.

A few seconds later, a man dressed in black stepped out of the trees and pulled up his zipper as he headed toward the house. As if suddenly sensing our presence, he lowered his hand to his hip and reached for his gun. The moment he found us, it was too late. My bullet had already taken his life as his body slumped to the ground.

We kept walking, slowly inching around the back of the house while listening for others. I knew they were bound to come rushing out as soon as they heard the gunshot. It wasn't like they didn't know we were there—the cameras had been tracking us since we got through the clearing and approached the house. It was only a matter of time before they sent someone for us, and that person would be ready to kill.

I heard a door slam shut ahead of me and waited. But before I could focus on the two heavily armored men heading my way, I heard a commotion behind me. Quinn gasped as a hand clamped around her mouth. The sound was enough to get my attention, and I spun around and fired another shot, missing Quinn's head by a fraction of an inch.

Her eyes widened, but she bit back the scream that was building inside. I could see the fear in her eyes, knowing how close the bullet had been to taking her life if I had missed my mark. Trust wasn't enough when you were faced with something like that. If it had been me, I likely would have pissed myself on the spot.

I didn't have time to ask if she was okay. I knew the other two men would round the corner and be on top of us in seconds. I raised my gun and waited like a hunter stalking their prey. It was us against them, and I was determined to make it out of here alive.

Just as expected, the two men came around the corner with tactical gear on and .45s pointing in our direction. I didn't turn to see what Quinn was shooting at when I heard her discharge her weapon. Instead, I transported myself back to being a sniper and took them out before they got off one shot. Once they were down and I didn't hear anyone else approaching, I spun around to find Quinn staring down at the three bodies lying on the ground less than twenty feet away from her.

"Nice shot," I commented, nodding my approval.

"Thanks. I don't think I've ever fired a gun this many times in my life," she joked. "It's a lot different than going to a stuffy warehouse and shooting at targets on the wall."

I noticed how her eyes clouded with tears and recognized the emotion running through her. The struggle of knowing that you'd taken a life while assuring yourself that if you didn't take theirs, they would have taken yours. It was an ugly feeling that would crawl into your brain and live in the depths of darkness, always waiting to rear its head when you least expected it.

"We need to keep moving," I said, keeping all emotion out of my voice. Now wasn't the time to feel anything. I had a job to do and needed to focus on that. Mission: Rescue Rosie.

"Okay," she whispered and pulled her shoulders back. She lifted her chin and gave me a quick nod, letting me know that she was ready.

We resumed our positions with me leading and her following behind me. As we circled around the house, we heard a few voices inside but nothing outside anymore. That didn't mean that we were truly alone; it just meant that they would find us before we found them.

"Find them and kill them," a woman shouted, her voice floating through an open window upstairs.

There was an order to kill, but I didn't know how many people it was given to. One? Two? Twenty? It was hard to know how big Julia's crew of goons was, but one thing was for sure—it would only be a matter of time before we would be greeted by more gunfire.

"I think we should separate," I whispered over my shoulder. "I'll take care of the goons; you get inside and find Rosie."

"Are you sure that's a good idea?" she asked nervously.

"I'll follow you in and cover you while you take the lead.

It's the only way to make sure we get to her before it's too late. If you come across anyone on your way to her, shoot them. Don't spare anyone. I'll handle the rest."

"Okay."

I took a deep breath, steadied my arms, and said a silent prayer before I kicked the door in and stepped aside to avoid the gunfire as it came flying at us.

Forty-Seven

Quinn

I had never seen this much gunfire in my entire life, including the gory, action-packed movies I watched with Justin before Rosie was born. I ducked and held my body against the door frame, glancing at Roman as I waited for his signal.

He stayed perfectly still with his AR15 held tightly against his chest. I wasn't sure if he was waiting for them to run out of ammo or if he was waiting for them to come outside looking for us. Either way, I wouldn't make a move without his direction.

A few minutes later, we heard heavy footsteps as a rush of armed men came flying through the door with guns drawn. Roman lifted his weapon at the perfect moment, jabbing the butt of it into one guy's face while I shot at another. It felt wildly reckless, but I kept an eye on Roman and shot at everyone else.

The bodies started falling around us as Roman continued shooting. He gave me a quick nod, stepped over their bodies, and went into the house. He rushed through and cleared the living room, then went into the kitchen while I took the stairs two at a time with my gun steady in front of me.

I heard a few shots downstairs but forced myself to keep moving toward the voices at the end of the hall. I was desperate to get to Rosie but knew that I couldn't be reckless. I listened carefully as I walked lightly, trying to keep my footsteps from being too heavy.

A floorboard creaked behind me, forcing me to spin around. I was face to face with a large, burly man whose face was covered in tattoos. He gave me a lopsided grin and pulled a knife from behind his back, swiping it at me as I jumped back. I narrowed my eyes and fired a shot, hating how many people I had now killed in one day.

His body swayed toward me as I jumped out of the way. I continued moving down the hallway and focused on the large bedroom at the far end. This was the room we had heard Rosie's voice from outside, so it felt like the first place I should look.

I slowly turned the knob and pushed the door open.

My heart leaped out of my chest into my throat, strangling the scream that threatened to come out when I saw Rosie sitting on a king-sized bed next to a man. Julia was sitting in a chair beside the bed, talking to them when they all looked up at me.

"Mama!" Rosie shrieked, jumping up to get off of the bed.

"Not so fast," the man said, reaching over and putting her down beside him. "You're not going anywhere."

Rosie's face fell, and tears welled in her eyes.

I stared in disbelief at the image before me. The guy looked familiar, but I couldn't figure out why.

"Give me my daughter," I demanded, my voice quieter and weaker than intended. "Now."

"She's not your daughter anymore. I told you that on the phone earlier." Julia tossed her red hair over her shoulder and tilted her head. "She's not going anywhere."

Anger was boiling inside of me as I watched them. My finger itched to pull the trigger and take both of them out, but I didn't want to traumatize Rosie by shooting a bullet into the man sitting beside her. It would be loud, and there would be blood everywhere, which would upset anyone, let alone a five-year-old.

He turned to whisper something to Julia behind his hand, and I noticed a black serpent-looking tattoo on his neck. In an instant, I knew where I had recognized him from. He was Elias Salvador, the son of Juan Salvador, and part of the child trafficking ring Justin had shut down before he was killed.

"If I were you, I'd lower your weapon," Elias said with a heavy accent. "I wouldn't want you to upset my daughter."

"Don't you dare call her that," I bit out, my hands starting to tremble with anger as I kept my gun as steady as possible.

"It's your choice, but my men will be here in a minute to take care of this," he waved his hand in the air as if I were some mess on the street that needed to be cleaned up.

I watched the Rolex slide down his wrist before he lowered his hands into his lap again. He sat there, looking overly relaxed in his white silky button-down shirt and dress slacks that had been freshly pressed. He didn't look like he had a care in the world, and I knew that was all about to change as soon as Roman got there.

"I don't care about your men," I lied. "We've already taken the majority of them out."

"Is that so?" He smirked, and I wanted to punch the smile off his stupid face.

Where was Roman? I could only stall this guy for so long. We needed to get Rosie and get the hell out of there.

"Just give me my daughter, and I'll let you two get back to whatever this is," I said, pointing between him and Julia with my gun.

"Again, Rosie is our daughter, Quinn. Now leave." Julia

stood up from the chair and then immediately sat down when he nodded to her and shook his head.

So he was the one in control and calling all of the shots. That was helpful information to have.

"You know damn well that she's not your daughter. You're out of your fucking mind, Julia."

Silence lingered in the air for a few minutes as we stared at each other. Then he whispered something to her and nodded to me.

"Go on, tell her what happened. Explain why this child is owed to us."

I narrowed my eyes at him, then glanced at Rosie to make sure she was still okay. Overall she appeared to be, but that didn't mean anything. I wouldn't trust it until I could hold her in my arms and see for myself.

"Rosie was our daughter. She died six years ago. A car accident. You might remember it, Quinn."

My heart sank when I started putting the pieces together.

"You shouldn't be driving when you're this upset," I scolded Justin as he got into the car. "Just stay and talk to me about it. Please."

"There's nothing to talk about, Quinn. I love you. I love our life. But I don't know if I can do this. I don't know if I can be a good father."

He pulled the car door shut as I jumped away. Then he reversed out of the driveway, leaving me in a puddle of tears.

I had sat at home that night, waiting for him to return. After I got a call from the hospital, I rushed over and paced anxiously in the emergency room waiting area for an update on Justin.

My mind constantly got the worse of me as I thought about the worst that could happen. I couldn't imagine bringing a baby into this world without him by my side. He was my everything. I needed him.

When the doctors updated me a few hours later, I was relieved to hear he was conscious, stable, and expected to make a full recovery, though he would be going home with a few broken bones. He was going to be held overnight to make sure his vitals stayed stable, but overall, he was okay.

It wasn't until the next morning that he told me the accident had been his fault. He was distracted and hadn't noticed the light turning red. He went through the intersection, t-boning a minivan. He repeatedly apologized for leaving and promised he would never do it again.

When he asked me to get an update on the other people, I went searching for his nurse and asked if they were okay.

"Unfortunately, the mother is still in the ICU. We can't give out more information than that right now."

"The mother?" I asked as my heart beat wildly in my chest.

"Her daughter was in the backseat. She didn't make it."

When I shared the news with Justin, he cried and held his hand against my flat stomach, vowing to be the perfect father to our baby. I knew that he would never be the same after this and my heart shattered knowing that he would never forgive himself for taking an innocent child's life.

I remembered the night very well, and to this day, it still haunted my nightmares.

"Justin wasn't always a play-it-by-the-rules kind of guy," Julia said once she saw the look on my face. "His recklessness took my baby from me. He took the only thing that I ever loved. The only person who mattered to me."

"And now you're trying to take mine."

"No, Quinn. I'm taking back what was owed to me. Justin took my daughter, and now I'm taking his."

"It's not the same, Julia. You know that."

"As a mother, you know what it feels like to see your child hurting. How do you think I felt being pinned in the car, listening as my baby fought for her life? Hearing her gasp as she took her last breath. Not being able to get the words out to say that I loved her because I couldn't believe what was happening. Nothing can prepare you for that, Quinn. Nothing. Justin never had to pay for what happened. The police called it an accident. *An unfortunate accident.* But that doesn't make it right, and it's about time he paid."

"He's not here anymore. How do you expect him to pay? You're not getting revenge on Justin; you're taking your grief out on his innocent daughter."

"I tried to make it right while he was here!" she yelled, startling me. "I did everything that I could. He was a stubborn ass, and nothing could get through to him."

"Then accept that and move on. Taking his daughter won't fix anything, Julia. You need to see someone and get help."

"Now you sound like him," she scoffed. "*You need to go to therapy. This isn't healthy. You're crazy.*"

Her eyes widened, and she actually looked crazy as she said it.

"You talked to Justin about what happened?"

"He knew who I was as soon as I started working for the FBI. I could tell that he remembered what happened—how could he not? It hadn't been that long since it happened. He said he wished he could take everything back that night, and since he couldn't, he would find a way to make it right."

I tried to keep from rolling my eyes. That was the stupidest thing I had ever heard. There was no way to *make it right* when you took someone's life—especially a child. Though I imagined that the guilt was constantly eating away at him, I couldn't see what he could possibly do to fix what he had done. It wasn't like he could just give her a baby.

"Elias and I struggled to get pregnant with Rosie. She was a miracle baby, and we cherished every moment we had with her. Unfortunately, I sustained severe injuries in the accident that night, and the doctors confirmed that I wouldn't be able to carry another child. It would be too risky. But we wanted another child…."

Her voice trailed off and sent a chill up my spine.

"So you started kidnapping other people's children?" I bit out sourly.

"It's not really kidnapping when the parent doesn't want them." She shrugged. "There are plenty of parents who want to escape the burden of parenthood, and believe it or not, everyone has a price."

"Yeah, well, my daughter isn't for sale."

"Trust me; *everyone* has a price. But this isn't about that, now is it? Because we're not paying you for her. We're taking her. Taking what is owed to us."

"How do you figure that she's *owed* to you? Just because she has the same name as your child doesn't mean she's destined to be yours."

"Don't you get it?" Julia asked, leaning forward, and looking quizzically at me. "She is the perfect daughter for us. She's the same age that our Rosie was when she died. It's like picking up right where we left off."

I felt a whimper escape my throat and blinked rapidly, forcing the tears away from my eyes.

"No," I blurted out. "I'm not letting this happen."

"You don't have much of a choice, now do you? I tried to make it easier for you, Quinn. I tried to give you a heads-up that this was coming so you could be prepared. I figured you would be fine knowing that you still had a chance to start over with that new boyfriend of yours. You guys look so cozy together, don't they?" She turned and looked at Elias, waiting for his answer.

"The coziest."

"But unfortunately, you seem so determined to stop this, and now you know too much, so we're going to have to change plans."

She got up and opened the drawer on the nightstand between them.

"Why now?" I asked, trying to stall for a few more minutes. I knew that Roman was close, I could feel it in my bones. I trusted that he was staying in the shadows for a reason.

"Well, they actually tried to take her a few days ago, but it wasn't the right time," Julia laughed and pulled a gun out. She wiped it off with the bottom of her shirt and inspected it to make sure it shined the way she wanted it to. "I had forgotten the exact date until Elias told me. Everything had to be perfect. That's why we took her today. Today was *the* day."

"The day for what?"

"It was exactly six years ago today that our sweet Rosie died."

"This is ridiculous!" I shrieked. "You can't just take someone's child because yours died. Life doesn't work that way."

"It's not just that, Quinn. Justin ruined *everything* for me. Not only did he kill our daughter, he was constantly putting his nose where it didn't belong."

My stomach dropped when I realized where she was going with this.

"Yeah, that's right. After he convinced Ariel to confess, I knew that he was getting close. Too close. I hated him for pushing her so hard. If he would have backed off, we could have taken care of her the same way we take care of anyone who leaves before they're given permission. So many lives could have been saved. Like his."

I didn't want to ask, but the question flew out of my mouth before I could stop it.

"You killed my husband on purpose?"

She shrugged, then slowly, a malicious grin spread across her face.

"He had what was coming to him."

Elias crossed and uncrossed his ankles as his legs extended out in front of me. He sighed heavily as if he was bored with the conversation.

"Anytime now, my love," he replied, raising his brows at her.

I barely had time to see what was happening as Rosie sprung off the bed and charged at Julia. I screamed and watched in horror as her little body leaped into the air, her fists clenched as they swung at Julia before Elias jumped up and grabbed her.

"You killed my dad?!" she screamed furiously as he carried her over his arm across the room.

Fury blinded me as I stared at Julia. Before I could speak, I heard a woman's voice behind me.

"Put the gun down."

Julia narrowed her eyes and moved her aim from me to the girl now standing next to me.

I wasn't sure what was happening, but since they were aimed at each other, I turned and focused mine on Elias.

In a split second, gunfire rang out in the room and I took cover as I heard a bullet whip beside me. I spun around to find Roman in the hallway, rushing into the room.

Julia was on the floor in a puddle of blood, matching the mess Elias had made on the other side of the bed. Rosie was standing there, screaming, as red splattered her hair and face.

"Go get Rosie, Quinn," Roman instructed, rushing in and blocking me from the other woman.

"I'm not here to hurt anyone," she said, lowering her gun and handing it to Roman.

Forty-Eight

Roman

"Julia took me when I was seven. My mom was a drug addict and didn't care what happened to me. She just wanted that next fix. At first, I thought Julia was a godsend until I was old enough to know what they were doing."

"Why didn't you try to leave and get help?" Quinn asked as she held Rosie on her lap.

"I couldn't. Every time I tried, they caught me. By the time I was thirteen, Julia had started showing me the *ropes* and told me that if I didn't want that kind of life, then I could work for her. I didn't know what she meant at the time, but I knew that I didn't want the men to touch me anymore, so I agreed. She started teaching me how to lure children away and said we made the perfect team because I was someone they would trust."

"That's why I wanted to help Bree when she lost her puppy," Rosie said sadly, tucking her head into Quinn's shoulder.

"I'm sorry about that," Bree sighed. "I didn't want to do it. But I also didn't have a choice. Julia had changed once Elias came back. She wasn't nice to me anymore. I was afraid of what she might do to me after I saw what happened to Ariel. She told me to lead her away from the house, then got upset after I did because Elias reminded her that it wasn't the right day. They had been planning it for a while."

"We'll need you to talk to the police about this," Quinn said softly. "I'm here to help you however I can, but we need to make sure that there are no other victims that we don't know about. Was she working with anyone else?"

"No," Bree shook her head. "She hadn't done much while Elias was locked up. Once he was out, they became obsessed with Rosie and getting revenge on Justin for the accident and then for uncovering their operation. It was too risky for her to start it up again right away, and she didn't have all of the resources she needed. She was told to hire people to take out Justin's team so there were no traces back to her. She even hired people for other stuff, like breaking into your apartments." She looked between us. That explained the random thug that Quinn had shot in my apartment.

"That's why everyone on Justin's team was targeted and murdered," I commented, not letting on to whether Mike was alive or dead. "Except her."

She nodded.

"Yeah, but she was so desperate to stay off the radar that she hired someone to attack her."

That didn't surprise me any, given how crazy and desperate she had been.

"She hated him for what he did. That's all she ever talked about. There were pictures of Rosie on her walls in the other house, and she would talk to them daily. I started to worry that she was going crazy when she started adding new ones," she lowered her voice and nodded at Rosie. "She ended up bringing us to this cabin because she didn't want anyone to find Rosie and have them take her from them again. I don't know how long she was planning to stay here, but my guess is that none of us were ever leaving here again."

"Well, it's all over now," Quinn said. "The police should be here shortly, and then we can all get the hell out of this creepy cabin."

We all nodded and sat quietly at the table in the kitchen, one of the few places that didn't have dead bodies on the floor. Soon, we heard sirens in the distance and knew the police were headed our way.

"Thank you, by the way," Quinn added. "For stepping in earlier. Rosie told me you had talked to her and told her to fight. Thanks for looking out for her."

Bree smiled sadly and looked at Rosie.

"I didn't want this life for her. No one ever fought for me. I wanted to make sure that she had at least one person who would be there to fight for her if you couldn't get here."

Soon, the house was buzzing with activity as OMI worked on securing the crime scene. We stayed long enough for the mandatory interviews and agreed not to leave town. This was a huge investigation that would span across several agencies, so it was going to take some time before the case was closed. We said goodbye to Bree, and Quinn promised to check in on her as soon as she was able to. For now, she would go with child protective services and be placed into foster care until she turns 18.

Since we didn't want to steal another vehicle or be caught in the truck we had taken to get there in the first place, I called Trevor and asked for a ride.

Max's wedding was over a few hours ago, and Trevor had skipped out early to check on Mike for me. Instead of taking us to my apartment or Quinn's, he drove us to another remote cabin and assured me that it was still within the jurisdiction we agreed to stay in.

"How's he feeling?" Quinn asked from the backseat as we ventured down a bumpy, gravel road. Rosie was buckled in the seat next to her, asleep with her head on Quinn's shoulder.

"I'll let you see for yourself," Trevor said, putting the truck in park.

Forty-Nine

Quinn

Mike was asleep by the time Trevor dropped us off at the cabin last night. We quietly headed to the back, where a guest room had been made up for us. The place was much bigger than the last one we had stayed in, with three large rooms and two full bathrooms.

I didn't sleep much that night because I kept rolling over to make sure Rosie was still beside me. Roman slept on the other side of her, making sure she couldn't get away without one of us noticing. While the threat and danger of someone taking her was gone now that Julia had been arrested, it took some time to register that we didn't have to hover and watch her every move.

I rolled over and smiled at the sunlight streaming in through the window. Today was going to be a wonderful day. Roman and I were together. We had Rosie, and no one was going to take her. On top of that, my brother was safe and alive. What more could I have asked for?

"Good morning, Mommy," Rosie's small voice greeted me as she opened her eyes and looked at me.

"Good morning, sweet girl." I brushed a strand of hair off her forehead, trying to be quiet so we didn't wake up Roman.

"Good morning," Rosie said sleepily, smiling at him.

I looked over her to find him smiling at both of us.

"Good morning, Rosie."

"Can I go see Uncle Mike?" she asked, sitting up and whipping the covers off all of us.

I laughed at her excitement and nodded my head. "Just be careful; he's not usually a morning person," I called after her.

"I heard that," he yelled from the living room.

I smiled and climbed out of bed, groaning as I felt the ache and stiffness in my body.

"You okay?" Roman asked as he climbed out of bed, eyeing me suspiciously.

"Yeah," I laughed. "I'm not a spring chicken anymore. I'm more like an old, grumpy pterodactyl. Way too old to be running around like I'm a twenty-something hotshot chasing the bad guys."

My body was sore, and I could definitely use some Ibuprofen, a hot bath, and probably some Icy-Hot at this point.

"I'm feeling it today, too," he said with a smile.

"Sorry," I winced and scrunched my nose.

"Don't be. I would go through heaven and hell to get to you, Quinn. You and Rosie are everything to me, and there's nothing that would ever stop me. Not old age. Not a bad knee. Not even arthritis."

He came around the bed and wrapped me in his arms.

"I haven't had a chance to tell you how much I appreciate what you did—" I started before he lifted a finger to my lips and stopped me.

"You don't need to thank me, Quinn."

His finger fell to the side and gently brushed against my cheek as his lips lowered to mine.

I melted into him, feeling safe in his muscular arms. The kiss was too quick for my liking, but it wasn't like we had total privacy and could trust that Rosie wouldn't walk in on us. The last thing I wanted to do right now was explain my new relationship to her on top of everything else she had going on.

"We don't need to talk about what happened until you're ready," he murmured. "But please don't thank me. I did what I did because I love you, Quinn. More than I ever knew was possible. I love you, and I love Rosie as if she was my own child. It's a weird feeling, one that I wasn't sure I would ever feel, but I promise that I would do anything for that girl."

"I love you too, Roman. We both do. Rosie just adores you," I smiled, looking up into his eyes.

I thought about everything that happened last night and what Julia had confessed. I still had so much anger inside me that I couldn't see straight.

"What's wrong?" Roman asked, lifting my chin with his fingers as he noticed my mood shift.

"Nothing," I lied.

"Quinn…."

I shook my head and inhaled slowly.

"I can't stop thinking about finding Rosie in that room with Julia and Elias. I keep seeing red from the anger that makes me want to rip their heads off and kill them all over again. I know that Rosie is fine, but I can't stop thinking about what would have happened if I hadn't gotten there when I did. This world is a cruel, disgusting place…."

"Look at me," he coaxed, bringing my attention back to him. "Nothing is ever going to happen to her again. Not with two bad-ass old people watching out for her."

I felt my cheeks burn from the stupid smile that stretched across my face at him calling us old. It was true, which only made it even funnier.

"Maybe we should get a logo and start a team of bad-ass old people?" I suggested. "Make it a cool thing."

"Whatever your heart desires," he laughed and kissed my forehead.

Fifty

Roman

"Come on, it can't be that bad," I laughed, watching the scowl etch deeper on Mike's face as he watched Anastasia from across the room.

"She's here ALL. THE. TIME."

"Where else is she supposed to go?"

"I don't know, but I don't see why we have to be stuck in the same room constantly," he growled, shifting his gaze to where she was sitting in the kitchen by the window. "There are multiple rooms in this damn cabin, they could at least put her in another one at night so I don't have to hear her snore."

"Well, given that you both got shot by someone in your own department who tried to take out your entire team, it makes sense that you are both being protected in the same cabin. And since you both need medical attention and there's only one doctor, I imagine that it's a whole lot easier for him to focus when you're both in the same room at night, so he doesn't have to go back and forth throughout the house all night."

"It's not like the wounds are that bad. Her forehead was barely grazed, and the bullet went right through my shoulder. I'll be up and going again in no time."

"Either way, until all agencies have a chance to do their part of the investigation, you guys are stuck here together for a while."

He glared at me and then turned away to watch Rosie play outside.

"How's she doing?" he asked, nodding at her, and effectively changing the subject.

"She seems to be fine," I replied with a shrug. "I don't know that she's really processed what happened. Either that, or she's too young to know what it all means. Quinn's keeping an eye on her, though."

"And how is Quinn doing? She looks tired. Run down."

"She is. She's been through a lot and hearing the things Julia said is going to sit heavily on her mind for a while. But she'll be okay. I'll make sure of it."

He turned and studied me.

"So, this thing with my sister is the real deal?"

I exhaled heavily, my elbows resting on my knees as I thought about the answer. I'd never been a committed relationship kind of guy, and Mike knew that. It wasn't that I didn't want to be that for Quinn, but I didn't know how to talk about it. Mike had been my best friend for as long as I could remember, and this was his sister. It would forever be a line that I would cross as long as Quinn and I were together.

"It's the real deal, man. I love them. I would do anything to protect them."

He leaned back and smiled the first genuine smile I had seen from him in months.

"I'm happy for you," he said. "Just don't break her heart, or I'll break your legs."

"You'd have to catch me first," I joked, knowing neither of us was in any condition to be chasing anyone for a while.

Mike and I sat and talked for a while, bullshitting just like we used to before everything happened. Anastasia was busy with the doctor and stayed out of his way, even though he still groaned and bellyached every time she walked by. He could deny it all he wanted, but Quinn was right—he had a thing for her. The chemistry between them reminded me of what Quinn and I had fought against until we finally gave in.

By dinner, Quinn and Rosie had cooked and made a delicious meal that just happened to be Mike's favorite. I knew that Quinn felt guilty about Mike being shot, even though he told her repeatedly not to. Cooking seemed to be her language of love, which explained the feast before us.

Anastasia had offered to make herself a sandwich and eat outside until Quinn insisted that not only she join us for dinner but that she also sit next to Mike. I knew what she was up to and tried to bite back my laughter when Mike scowled at the suggestion.

"To friends and family," Quinn said, lifting her glass of water in the air. Everyone raised their glasses in response before we dove into the delicious meal in front of us. It felt good to relax and know that there was no longer anything to worry about.

252

Epilogue

Quinn

4 Weeks Later

"Is all of this stuff going to fit in here?" I asked with my hand on my hip as I looked around at the boxes scattered throughout the room.

"We'll make it," Roman said, slipping his arm around my waist and planting a kiss on my forehead as he walked past me.

I studied all of the boxes, wondering how we had accumulated so much stuff, then remembered that not all of it was ours. Some were Roman's, which made me feel somewhat better. Still, we had a ton of stuff we didn't need, and now was a great time to get rid of it.

"Where do you want us to get started?" my mom asked as she walked through the front door with my sister Sonia.

"You guys didn't have to come help us unpack." I hugged them and looked helplessly at the mess around us.

"I live next door; it's not like I had to go far," my mom laughed. "Plus, we're family, and we help out. Now, where do you want us?"

Roman and I had barely started entertaining the idea of moving in together when the house next to my mom went up for sale. It was easier than going back and forth between apartments all the time, and Rosie didn't seem to love the constant shuffling about. Not only that, I didn't feel comfortable in either apartment anymore, and that bothered me more than I was willing to let on.

As soon as my mom mentioned that it was on the market, we didn't waste any time making an offer. Before we knew it, it was ours, and we were moving in. Neither of us had any issues saying goodbye to our apartments and were able to get out of our leases reasonably easily. It was New York City and there were dozens of people looking for a place to live after moving to the big city and chasing after their dreams.

"Well, in that case…." I laughed. "How about the kitchen? All of the boxes are already in there. That way, we have plates to use for dinner tonight."

"We're on it," Sonia assured me with a pat on my back then they disappeared down the hallway to say hello to Rosie, who was busy unpacking her toys. We had already spent the morning getting her room set up so she could have time to play while we did all of the boring stuff.

I started sorting the other boxes into piles based on the rooms they went to. My goal was to set up both bathrooms and the kitchen today, then work on the living room, our bedroom, and the garage tomorrow. Our room had a bed, and that was about it right now, but Roman assured me that we didn't need anything else. He might have also wiggled his eyebrows and hinted at how he couldn't wait to christen the new room once Rosie went over to my mom's for a bit tomorrow so we could work on the final unpacking before going back to work on Monday.

It was wonderful being next to my mom, especially since Rosie was starting summer break this week, and I still had to push my way back into my boss's good graces after missing so much work lately. Luckily, once it was uncovered that Julia had been actively targeting everyone on Justin's team, he eased up some on me. They also found that she had joined the FBI shortly after she met Elias because he wanted someone on the inside to make sure his operation stayed off of the radar. Julia's mom had abandoned her at a young age, and she was easily impressionable, which made it easier for them to pull her into the organization. After her daughter was killed, she went off the deep end and became obsessed with replacing her, no matter the cost.

I had been in therapy for three weeks now, and Rosie was also seeing a therapist twice a week at Roman's encouragement. Even though things had settled down, I found that I had a lot of things that I still needed to process when it came to Justin and the secrets Julia had revealed that I hadn't known about him. Knowing that Rosie would be right next door at my mom's house gave me a sense of security that I hadn't been aware I needed.

The front door opened, and I looked up to find Mike walking in with a shit-eating grin. He had his hands behind his back as he tried to hide something big.

"What are you up to?" I asked, frowning.

"You'll see." He arched a brow and then called for Rosie.

She came bouncing down the hallway a few minutes later, rushing over to him when she stopped and remembered to be gentle with him. His recovery was going well, but he still wasn't 100%.

"Hi, Uncle Mike!" She wrapped her arms around his waist and hugged him.

"Hey, pumpkin butt."

"I don't have a pumpkin butt," she giggled, then looked over her shoulder to check.

He laughed and waited for her to ask what was behind his back. Roman came into the living room and wrapped an arm around my shoulders as my mom and Sonia joined us.

"Why are you standing so funny?" she asked, looking up at him.

"Because I have something special for you," he said, looking from her to me cautiously.

"You do? What is it?"

"Close your eyes."

She did as asked and waited patiently.

Mike brought his hand in front of him and set a small brown dog kennel on the floor.

"Open your eyes," he said.

Her eyes fluttered open, then she looked from him to the floor and jumped back.

"Is that what I think it is?"

Her voice was small and squeaky, eyes wide as she watched him.

"Why don't you check and see?"

Slowly she kneeled down and peered inside. She looked back up at him for approval before turning the lock and opening the door.

A tiny brown and white dog came bouncing out and into her arms. She picked it up and held it against her chest as the puppy excitedly licked her face.

"A puppy?!"

I raised a brow and pretended to be mad at him. The truth was that I wasn't. Roman and I had talked about getting a dog for Rosie since she had wanted one so badly before everything happened. He shrugged and looked sheepishly down at the floor. I knew my brother well enough to know that he was likely beating himself up now and second-guessing whether he had overstepped by getting her a dog without asking us first.

"What are you going to name it?" I asked, looking from Mike down to Rosie.

She pulled it away from her body and looked to see if it was a boy or a girl.

"This is Honey," she said, then lifted the dog to her face and kissed its nose.

"Welcome to the family, Honey," I said, feeling Roman's fingers as they held me a little tighter.

My life had changed a lot in a very short time, but I could finally say that for once, I was happy and exactly where I wanted to be. I had a man who loved me, a daughter who lit up my world, and now a puppy that was peeing on our brand-new rug. Life couldn't get any better than this.

****

Want to see what's happening with Mike? Check out his story here: https://books2read.com/u/4DKMoP

Looking for more action? Check out my steamy, small-town romantic suspense series packed full of action and heat!

Start 'Til Death Do Us Part Here (Haven Brook Book 1) here: https://books2read.com/u/m2RJNR

Want updates on new releases and sales? Be sure to subscribe to my newsletter so you don't miss anything! Newsletter: http://eepurl.com/g0NcSj

Other Books By Samantha Baca

<u>The Haven Brook Series:</u>

'Til Death Do Us Part (Haven Brook Book 1)

https://books2read.com/u/m2RJNR

The Cradle Will Fall (Haven Brook Book 2)

https://books2read.com/u/b6O0QE

The Ties That Bind (Haven Brook Book 3)

https://books2read.com/u/mqgoz8

A Very Haven Christmas (Haven Brook Book 4- Novella)

https://books2read.com/u/mvqGjj

Three Strikes, You're Gone (Haven Brook Book 5)

https://books2read.com/u/mvqL2z

<u>The Dark Shadows Series</u>

Five Steps Ahead (Dark Shadows Book 1)

https://books2read.com/u/38Q0gO

Ten Seconds Too Late (Dark Shadows Book 2)

https://books2read.com/u/3JRgVB

Against The Clock (Dark Shadows Book 3)

https://books2read.com/u/m2YwoR

Out Of Time (Dark Shadows Book 4)

https://books2read.com/u/4DKMoP

<u>The Stone Creek Series (Novellas)</u>

Chocolate Covered Mistletoe (Stone Creek Book 1)

https://books2read.com/u/3LRk9N

Candy Coated Promises (Stone Creek Book 2)

https://books2read.com/u/mldP5Y

Pumpkin Spiced Possibilities (Stone Creek Book 3)

https://books2read.com/u/bojdwV

Beaumont Creek Series

Just One Time (Beaumont Creek Book 1)

https://books2read.com/u/3G52zK

Second Chances (Beaumont Creek Book 2)

https://books2read.com/u/4Aj6Z0

Third Time's The Charm (Beaumont Creek Book 3)

https://books2read.com/u/b5lEyG

Four-ever Single (Beaumont Creek Book 4)

Preorder link coming soon

Fifth Wheel (Beaumont Creek Book 5)

Preorder link coming soon

Standalone Books

One Last Wish

https://books2read.com/u/mqg7D9

Finding Love In Apartment 2C (Novella)

https://books2read.com/u/bze9aZ

Cocky Counsel: A Hero Club Novel

https://books2read.com/u/31Kzkn

Something To Talk About

https://books2read.com/u/4X62ag

All Is Fair In Food And War

https://books2read.com/u/bp8qjX

Holiday Books

Snow Place To Go

https://books2read.com/u/4A560N

A Christmas Wish

https://books2read.com/u/4EKXpE

Blame It On The Mistletoe

https://books2read.com/u/bw1rqe

Holiday Hijinks

https://books2read.com/u/4DP6Ze

Acknowledgments

If you're still reading and have taken the time to read my acknowledgments, thank you! I appreciate your commitment and enthusiasm for my books! Be sure to find me on social media because I'm pretty sure this just made us best friends. So come stalk me, mkay? Okay!

Thank you to all the readers who continuously support me and grab my books as soon as they go on preorder. I cannot begin to express the love and gratitude that I have for you. I hope that you'll continue to stick with me on this adventure and that I can continue to bring you the stories you'd like to see.

My alpha readers—Azucena, Niki, and Amanda—I seriously don't know what I would do without you ladies. This book was a beast, and there were sooo many times that I threatened to toss it in the trash and write something else. Thank you for your never-ending support and words of encouragement when I needed them the most. Also, thanks for not judging me with some of the crap I wrote along the way....

Dear beta readers, my books would never be the same without you. Katy, Adrianna, and Kristen—you all took this book, helped me figure out what was still missing, and guided me to where I needed to improve it. Thank you for your honest feedback and for sharing your love for this series with me! You ladies are the best!!

Have I mentioned how much I love my ARC readers? I'm pretty sure I could post a grocery list up for review, and they would jump on it and remind me to get toilet paper because who doesn't need that? I am constantly blown away by the amount of support that I have and how many readers share their love for my books. Thank you for taking a chance on this book, I hope you enjoyed it!

My family will always be my biggest support, and I love that they're always there when I need them. My sweet girls are getting older, yet they're always just as excited when my books come in for the first time. I hope you both always have that passion for books and that reading continues to be an escape for you when you need it! I love you girls so much and couldn't imagine a world without you in it.

Richard—aka Mr. Do It All—thank you for staying by my side and not divorcing me when I make crazy goals for the year! I appreciate all of the help you always give me, whether it's working through a blurb or helping me bring a cover to life—you do it all, and I'm forever thankful for you.

To my readers—thank you. I love you! Stay the amazing people you are, and never lose that love for reading!

About the Author

Samantha lives in the southwest with her husband and two small children after abandoning her childhood dream of living in a cabin in Colorado when she found that she couldn't afford to live there and was deathly allergic to the woods. When she's not writing, she's usually spouting off sarcastic remarks while drinking wine out of a coffee mug to look like a functional adult while chasing down her toddlers. She enjoys spending time with her family, watching reruns of Friends, and the 24/7 flow of coffee that can be found in her veins. Be sure to follow her on social media for updates on what she's working on.

You can find her here:

Facebook: https://www.facebook.com/AuthorSamanthaBaca

Instagram: https://instagram.com/author_samantha_baca

Goodreads: http://www.goodreads.com/authorsamanthabaca

Facebook Reader Group:

https://www.facebook.com/groups/2945710968775398/

Webpage: https://authorsamanthabaca.wordpress.com

Newsletter: http://eepurl.com/g0NcSj